Ripple Effects

Ripple Effects

A Northern Woods Romance

Amy Hepp

FIFTH
AVENUE
PRESS

Fifth Avenue Press is a locally focused and publicly owned publishing imprint of the Ann Arbor District Library. It is dedicated to supporting the local writing community by promoting the production of original fiction, nonfiction, and poetry written for children, teens, and adults.

First Printing 2024

Layout: Ann Arbor District Library

Cover Illustration and Design: Nathaniel Roy

Editor: Kelsey Walker

ISBN: 978-1-956697-31-5 (Paperback); 978-1-956697-32-2 (Ebook)

Fifth Avenue Press

343 S Fifth Ave

Ann Arbor, MI 48104

fifthavenue.press

For Dan. My love, my muse, my forever.

Chapter One

FUNERALS WEREN'T PAYING GIGS, but when the dearly departed requested your voice at her last party on Earth, how could you say no?

The five-hour drive to Misty Lake, Minnesota, was nearing its end, and Penny exited the highway. She reached into her purse to dig out her phone for GPS to guide her the rest of the way, because one wrong turn could land her in the middle of a lake in the Boundary Waters. She shoved aside her hairbrush and crumpled a receipt.

After a quick glance at the road in front of her, she peeked into her purse. She pulled out her lipstick then tossed it back in and growled. Another look into her purse revealed her phone. When her hand wrapped around it, she looked back up at the road. The rear bumper of a luxury sedan filled her view. She slammed down on the breaks, but her worn brake pads squealed in protest—she bumped into the car.

"Shit, shit, shit," she muttered as she pulled to the side of the road behind the black sedan. The clock on the dashboard ticked at a furious pace. The funeral would begin in thirty minutes, and she needed to be there for the opening hymn.

She unbuckled and pushed herself out of her car. A quick look at her front bumper failed to help her identify the new dent amongst all the other dings, but when she turned to look at the other car, a gouge as bright as a diamond shining in the sun glared from the trunk of the sedan. The back door of the luxury vehicle opened, and a man's long legs emerged. He was dressed in a tailored, blue suit and brown dress shoes. She rolled her eyes at the outfit—it must have been worth more than her car. The walking fashion ad with wavy, brown hair removed his mirrored sunglasses and approached her.

"I'm soooo sorry," said Penny. "I needed my phone for directions because, you know, driving around these lakes is a nightmare, and it was buried at the bottom of my purse. You came out of nowhere, and I didn't see you, but I think it's just a little scrape." Penny rubbed her fingers against the scratch in an effort to buff out the damage. "How about I give you some money for the repairs? I'll grab my purse."

Penny hustled back to her car and yanked her purse off the passenger seat. The man still hadn't said anything. He stood there with a crooked smile plastered on his face as she plopped her purse on the trunk of the scarred car and dug around for money.

Her cluttered purse mirrored her current life—she chastised herself for not using a wallet like a normal person. Sweat trickled down her back, and after what seemed like an hour of digging, she finally found some cash. She thrust two twenties, a five, and two ones into the guy's hand. Would forty-seven dollars cover a gouge repair? She didn't have the guts to ask him. "Listen," she said, "I'm like, really, *really* late. I gotta go. Are we cool?"

The guy's face broke out into a full smile, a double dimple

appearing on his cheek. He straightened the crumpled bills into smooth rectangles before organizing them by amounts. She braced for harsh words from him, but instead, he placed the bills back into her hand and said, "Are you alright?"

Penny blinked. His voice—so gentle and smooth—could lull her to sleep. He must be a late-night DJ on the radio. Or maybe a pilot—their buttery voices reassured skittish passengers on planes. "Yeah, yeah. I'm fine."

"Are you sure your car is okay? Can I give you a lift?"

Penny glanced back at her beat-up car and then swiveled back toward the luxury sedan, whose air conditioning probably worked all the time. She waved her hand. "No, no. I'm fine. All good here."

"Well then, have a safe trip." The silky words flowed from his lips—she didn't move until the closure of his car door jerked her out of her trance. In a motion as smooth as his voice, she grabbed her purse off the trunk of the sedan before it drove off the shoulder.

* * *

"Everything alright, Mr. Young?" the driver asked Beckett as they pulled away from the scene.

Beckett Young turned back to catch another glimpse of the lithe redhead with the huge purse. "Everything's fine. She's not hurt, and it's a small scratch. You can drive to the church now." He leaned his head back on the soft seat as his driver wound around the lakes and approached the only stop light in Misty Lake, Minnesota. Beckett breathed in through his nose and out of his mouth. He repeated the action until his nerves calmed.

The driver slowed as the concrete road turned into a brick road, which surrounded an oval-shaped park in the middle of town. Beckett peered out of the tinted window as they navigated around the circle. Tall trees and benches dotted the park, a free-standing clock stood on the edge of the grassy circle, and what was left of a gazebo sat in the middle of the space. Residents crossed from one side of the town to the other using the sidewalks that ran through the park. As Beckett's driver rounded the oval, the hearse came into view along with his cousins' cars. He swallowed hard.

Beckett glanced at his watch. "We're early," he said to the driver.

"Would you like me to drive through town again?"

"Yes, please." He dreaded facing Aunt Helen's children and grandchildren. It'd been three weeks since the accident, and he still hadn't slept without nightmares. Food didn't appeal to him, and he couldn't even wrap his brain around returning to work on Monday.

His temple throbbed as the car drove back around the park and down a side street away from the church. Homes with big front yards shaded by tall trees filled the streets in the small town. Two young girls played hopscotch on the wide sidewalk, and a couple pushed a stroller. A teenager mowed a lawn next to an old man washing his car. The normalcy eased his racing heart. Beckett blew out a breath and slumped against the buttery leather seat. He still couldn't believe his beloved Aunt Helen was gone.

By the time Penny shoved the loose bills back into her unwieldy purse and found her way around the lakes, there were ten minutes left before the funeral service. Late again and no time for a proper warm-up, she ran through her breathing exercises and vocalizations at the one stop light in Misty Lake.

When the green light flashed, she whipped around the

center of town and parked her car on a side street. She grabbed her purse and ran up the sidewalk, weaving around the mourners heading into the church for the funeral. Sweat dripped down her back as she hustled through a side door. Her heels slid along the tile floor, and her friend, Emma, paced the hallway.

"Where have you been?" said Emma in a loud whisper. "The service starts in five minutes. Helen's family wanted to meet you before it began, but it's too late now."

In the previous summer, Penny met Emma on a guided canoe camping trip with the Northern Woods lodge. Emma was like the big sister she never had, and Helen—a sixty-something badass—was the only other woman on the trip. Helen shared her camping expertise and life wisdom as they navigated the lakes and portages of the Boundary Waters. Penny couldn't believe Helen was gone, but she was grateful her family requested her voice at the funeral.

"Sorry. Traffic." She thrust her purse into Emma's arms and dug around for her tube of lipstick. She found it on the first grab and applied the fresh color to her lips. Penny fluffed her long, curly, auburn hair and said to Emma, "How do I look?"

Emma rolled her eyes. "Flawless as usual. You better get inside." Emma opened the side door to the sanctuary. Penny folded her hands and walked to the metal chair beside the organ. The organist nodded to her and continued his prelude while ushers worked to find seats for the mourners in the small church. Helen's four adult children asked for the Misty Lake church to host the funeral service since it was close to the cemetery Helen requested. Her last wish was to spend eternity near the Boundary Waters.

The minister proceeded to the altar behind the casket while the organist played the introduction of the opening hymn. Penny stood and inhaled a deep breath before the first phrase. When her mezzo-soprano voice filled the space, attendees pulled cloth hankies from purses and blotted their faces—the occasional nose blow accompanied her solo. The last note hung in the air, and when she opened her eyes, the congregation stilled. Penny sat on the metal chair beside the organist as the minister thanked her for the hymn and proceeded with the service.

Helen's children and grandchildren filled the first three rows while Penny scanned the crowd for Emma. She found her sitting with her fiancé, Mark Gere, and the rest of their camping friends from their trip in the fifth row. Her gaze strayed to a man in the back pew. *Crap.* What was he doing at Helen's funeral?

The guy with the sexy voice from the luxury sedan caught her staring. He raised his eyebrow and gave her a little wave. Penny slid down in her seat and avoided any further eye contact while the minister offered prayers, a message, and love for their departed friend, Helen.

Penny led the congregation through the final hymn as Helen's casket journeyed up the aisle on the shoulders of her family. The organist played one more piece, and Penny waited until he finished before leaving her seat.

"Pretty good for no warm-up," said the organist.

"Thanks. Sorry. Traffic."

The organist gathered his music. "If you're ever back in town, give me a call. I'd love to have you sing for services." He offered his business card to her.

Penny forced a smile and palmed the card. "Thanks." Church services weren't her first choice for gigs, but she took anything these days. A week ago, she sang 1950s top hits for a high school class celebrating its seventieth reunion. The twenty-three people in attendance appreciated her efforts, but it was a long afternoon.

The organist ducked out of the side exit while Penny walked down the center aisle and out of the double wooden doors. Her eyes adjusted from the dark interior of the church to the bright sky of an early September day in the Boundary Waters. Wind blew her black, polyester dress against her thighs as she scanned the crowd for Mark and Emma. She found them on a grassy area near the side of the church with the rest of their friends from the trip. As she approached the small group, Emma handed over her purse.

"Thanks," said Penny as she stuffed the organist's business card into her purse. Conversation flowed around her, but her gaze was pulled across the churchyard to the park in the center of town. "What's going on with the gazebo?" The roof and half of the support beams were in a heap on the ground beside the structure.

"The wood rotted, and the town voted to tear it down and replace it with a pergola," said Emma.

"Cool."

"There's a reception with food at Northern Woods," said Emma. "Do you have time for a visit? Or do you need to head back home?"

Penny hadn't eaten in hours, and she didn't need to hurry home to her parents' house in Rochester, Minnesota. She had moved back home after her college graduation and hustled gigs in her hometown to build up her savings. The gigs were steady, but she couldn't afford to strike out on her own yet. She helped her mom with the dishes and slept in her childhood bed every night like in high school. Her dream to sing and dance on Broadway perched at the top of a tall ladder, and she remained on the bottom rung. "I can stay for a while."

"If it gets late, you can crash with us. We have a guest room upstairs. You should stay anyway—our Labor Day barbecue is tomorrow."

The group parted. Penny returned to her car and found a parking ticket flapping in the breeze on her windshield. The ticket accused her of parking in front of a fire hydrant, though a bush blocked the fire hydrant in question. She stuffed the ticket into her glove box with her other unpaid infractions—she'd worry about them later.

The short drive to Northern Woods took her through town and then a mile down a dirt road. Cars and trucks jammed the parking lot. Penny didn't see any fire hydrants, so she maneuvered her dented car in between two pickup trucks and then climbed the steps of the Northern Woods lodge.

Finger food filled the buffet, and tables were removed from the dining hall to accommodate the large group. Penny took a plate from the stack and filled it with the homemade goodness of Northern Woods. She wove through the crowd to where Mark and Emma stood by the large picture window, and she popped a mini quiche into her mouth. The flaky crust melted against her tongue. "Who's cooking here these days?" she asked.

"Her name is Kelly," said Emma. "She started here after our trip last summer. Her sous chef is amazing too, but Kelly bakes all the desserts. Sweets are her specialty."

After two more mini quiches and a handful of chicken tenders, Penny wiped her hands on a napkin. "I'm gonna grab some fresh air by the lake. Be back in a few."

Penny snagged two brownies from the dessert offerings before heading outside. The breeze blew her hair as she walked down the hill. Memories from last summer's Northern Woods canoe trip engulfed her. She allowed herself a moment of nostalgia on the bench by the lake where water lapped the rocks as a couple paddled by in a red canoe. She ate one of the brownies and moaned.

"That good, huh?" The smooth voice swept over her like a

lake breeze on a summer morning. She turned to her left and saw the man who rode in the back of the fancy sedan standing beside the bench. The lake reflected in his sunglasses. "May I join you?" he asked.

"Sure." She scooted over to make room for the stranger. The bench dipped when he sat beside her.

"Um, should we settle up?" she asked. "I can give you cash, or you can send me a bill for your car?" She held her breath. She didn't want to ask her parents for money to fix some guy's car. Maybe he'd work out a payment plan with her.

He shook his head. "I don't want your money. When my car pulled into the parking lot, you were walking down the hill. I didn't want you to leave before I had a chance to thank you. My Aunt Helen would've loved your beautiful voice during her service. Thanks."

"Helen was your aunt? I'm so sorry for your loss. She was awesome. Her kids asked me to sing, and I couldn't say no." She glanced at the man beside her, watching anguish cloud his face. Penny split her other brownie in half and offered the piece to him. Their fingers grazed as he accepted the sweet treat—she flinched.

He popped the sweet morsel into his mouth. "Thanks."

Penny brushed the brownie crumbs from her dress, and a wailing call sounded over the lake.

"What was that?" asked the man.

"A loon," said Penny. "Your Aunt Helen loved loons—the call of the north woods."

* * *

Beckett stared at the lake and adjusted the sunglasses on his face to hide the tears pooling in his eyes. The young woman, whose singing voice warmed him like a cashmere scarf on a cold night, sat silent on the bench beside him until a cloud passed in front of the sun. She bid farewell and hiked up the hill toward the lodge. The cloud moved, and the sun warmed his face.

The bench dipped, and his chest squeezed, hoping to see the curly redhead again. But when he turned, he found Helen's eldest daughter sitting beside him.

"Why didn't you sit with us in church?" she asked.

He shook his head. "You needed to be together."

"You're our family. We wanted you with us."

He blew out a breath and faced his cousin. "I'm sorry. It was all my fault."

"She had a bad heart."

"But I should've . . ."

"It was her time." His cousin patted him on the hand. "No one blames you."

"I'm so sorry." He whispered before he bolted from the bench and jogged up the hill to the car. He managed to avoid any further interactions with his cousins and sighed as he slid into the back seat of the sedan.

"Duluth airport. Thank you," he said to the driver. The driver didn't question him and pulled out of the gravel drive. Once they reached the highway, the smooth ride and air conditioning calmed his pulse and cooled his body but didn't rid him of the shame that consumed him since Helen's accident.

Chapter Two

THE BROWNIES GAVE Penny a boost of energy. She hiked up the hill, her heels creating divots in the grass. The grieving nephew stayed on the bench beside the lake, and Penny breathed a sigh of relief knowing he didn't want money for the scratch on his car. She didn't have a ton of extra cash lying around to fix some guy's ride anyway. Emma and Mark were still talking to their friends in the dining hall when Penny returned.

"I should get going," Penny said to the group. "It's a five-hour drive."

Emma clasped her arm. "I wish you'd stay the night. Our barbecue is tomorrow, and it'll be so much fun. Do you have a gig scheduled?"

"Not 'til next weekend." Last week's high school reunion was her last paying gig. Her cash reserves were low, and she needed to apply for a retail or desk job if things didn't pick up soon. Her parents didn't charge her rent, but she chipped in for food and paid for her own gas and car insurance. The money from her checking account flowed out like water. So, a party might be fun. She could use a break from the daily stress and anxiety. "Okay. I'll stay the night."

Penny followed Mark and Emma to their home, which sat behind the outfitter store Mark purchased last fall. As they parked in the store's parking lot, Penny surveyed the shop. A blue and white sign hung over the door—it read 'Mark's Gere.'

Penny snickered at the word play on Mark's last name. "Nice," said Penny.

"Thanks," said Mark.

The walk along the short path behind the store led them to a log cabin home with a wide front porch and a view of a private lake. Thick woods surrounded the property and shaded the home. She stood on the porch and inhaled the clean air. The lakes of the Boundary Waters reminded her of childhood vacations—they always calmed her.

"Do you see loons on your lake?" she asked Emma.

"No. Our lake isn't big enough, but we can hear them in the distance sometimes."

"Lucky."

Penny followed Mark and Emma inside. She wandered around the great room while they changed out of their dress clothes from the funeral.

Masculine furniture dominated the space, but Emma's feminine touches accented the room. A vase of fresh flowers adorned the coffee table while a colorful throw rested on the leather couch. A lamp on a side table cast a muted glow, and framed photos lined the mantle.

Penny picked up a photo of their camping team from last summer. Helen's wide and confident smile contrasted Mark and Emma's goofy grins. Penny raised her arms in the picture like she didn't have a care in the world. The Penny in the photo was about to begin her last year in college—things like car insurance and a steady income were a distant thought. She missed those days.

"A lot has changed in a year," said Emma as she approached Penny.

"For sure. Last Labor Day, I rearranged my schedule so I didn't have a class on Fridays. This Labor Day, I'm a college graduate and need to figure out my life. Mark quit his job as a CPA and bought the outfitter store, and you moved north from Chicago and got engaged." Penny set the photo back down on the mantle and sighed. "And Helen passed."

Emma nodded. "Come upstairs, and I'll show you the guest room."

Penny followed Emma into a pale blue room with a queen bed and framed photos of the Boundary Waters on the wall. A lamp and scented candle sat on a bedside table. Her purse landed with a thud on the bed. "I don't know if I'll ever be grown up enough to have a guest room."

Emma laughed and showed her the bathroom down the hall, but Penny wasn't kidding. The gigs were few and far between, and she couldn't live in her parents' house forever. What was she going to do?

The rich aroma of coffee woke Penny in the quiet blue room. Emma preferred tea, but Mark loved his coffee. Jackpot. She skipped downstairs in the shorts and T-shirt she kept in her purse for emergencies. She found Emma drinking tea and reading a book at the long, wooden dining table adjacent to the kitchen.

"Thanks for letting me crash here last night. Your house is amazing." Penny poured herself a cup of coffee. She stirred in three creams and a teaspoon of sugar.

"You can stay as long as you'd like. We love it here. It's private and peaceful."

"Nice. Are you still teaching?"

"No." Emma stared off into space. "I loved teaching the multi-grade level classroom in a small town on the Lake Superior coast. I'll miss the families, but Mark and I want to build our life together in Misty Lake. I resigned after the school year and moved in with Mark before the Fourth of July. I might apply for a teaching job in Misty Lake next year after the wedding. We'll see. Right now, I teach camping classes in the store and love it."

Penny nodded as she grabbed a loaf of bread and jam from the fridge. She slipped a piece of bread into the toaster and sipped the rich coffee. "Mark's a wizard with the coffee maker."

"He grinds his own beans. A total mess."

"Worth it." Penny slathered her toast with jam and took a big bite. "Hey, I meant to ask yesterday. How did Helen, you know...die?"

Emma sipped her tea and set her cup down on the saucer. "She had trouble with her heart, but we don't know. Mark learned of her passing from the staff at Northern Woods."

"I wish I could've chilled with her around a campfire one last time to soak up more of her life lessons."

"I know. I wanted her to come to our wedding. I'll miss her."

Penny finished her toast and swiped the crumbs off the table.

"I'm going to run into town to buy food for the barbecue. You can come with me if you want."

"I'm gonna grab a shower first." She gulped the rest of her coffee. After a quick shower and shampoo, she slipped her wet hair into a messy ponytail and brushed her teeth with the new toothbrush Emma had left for her on the counter.

She skipped back down the stairs, but a quiet moan stopped her on the landing. When she peeked around the corner, Mark held Emma in a tight embrace—their lips fit together in an open-mouth kiss. Emma's hand traveled to Mark's behind, and his fingers threaded through her hair.

Penny rolled her eyes. Geez. She couldn't remember the last time a guy ran a hand through her hair. Six months? A year? Her busy schedule left no time for a relationship, but her body remembered the feeling. Penny's core softened during Mark and Emma's embrace.

Their kiss deepened. When Mark's hand cupped Emma's breast, Penny ran back up the stairs and retreated to the bathroom. She slammed the door, flushed the toilet, and washed her hands. Satisfied she'd announced her arrival, she skipped down the stairs again. This time, Emma hid her face behind the newspaper and sipped her tea while Mark stood at the stove and stirred a sauce for the barbecue.

Families and couples arrived in the mid-afternoon—they spread out on the lawn and in the lake at Mark and Emma's house. A few brave souls swam in the chilly September water, an older man organized a fishing contest, families played lawn games, and teenagers paddled canoes on the lake. Penny sat in a lawn chair with a hot dog and chips on a paper plate. A cold beer nestled in the grass beside her. A woman with bouncy, blonde curls pulled up a chair and joined her.

"Hi. I'm Kelly."

Penny wiped her mouth with her napkin and nodded. "Penny O'Brien."

"How do you know Mark and Emma?"

"We did a Boundary Waters trip last summer through Northern Woods."

"I'm the chef at Northern Woods, but I wasn't hired until last fall."

Penny nodded. "The food at the funeral reception was great, but the desserts were delicious."

Kelly blushed. "Thanks. It was an honor to prepare the food for Helen's memorial service. I only met her once, but she was a neat lady. Are you in town long?"

"No. Emma convinced me to stay for her barbecue. The girl loves a party."

Kelly laughed. "You're right."

A tall, blond man—wearing pressed khakis and a striped golf shirt—carried a mounded plate of food and approached the women. He sank down in a chair beside Kelly and kissed her cheek. She offered him a chip, and his eyes twinkled at her gesture. Penny returned her attention to her hot dog.

"Glad you took an afternoon off work," said Kelly to the man. "Penny, this is my boyfriend, Drew." To the tall blond, she said, "This is Penny O'Brien. Mark and Emma's camping trip friend."

"Nice to meet you," Drew said to Penny.

"What do you do if you work on holidays?" asked Penny.

"I bought a law practice and home in town last winter, but the business was a mess. I've worked for months, and I still have a ton of boxes to plow through. I need help."

Penny didn't have a gig until next weekend. Plowing through boxes sounded easy enough. "You hirin'?"

Drew lifted his eyebrows. "Interested?"

"I'd have to ask Mark and Emma if I could crash for a few more days and borrow a T-shirt or two, but I'm all in for a short-term project."

"My office is on Elm Street." He handed her a business card. "If you're game, stop by tomorrow. I'll put you to work and pay you in cash."

"Great. Thanks." She slipped the card into the pocket of her shorts, got up, and dumped her trash in the bin. A week in the Boundary Waters beat loafing around her parents' house and trolling for gigs any day.

A plume of dust filled the air as Penny emptied boxes and sorted files in Drew's office. She spent the morning alphabetizing and organizing the filing cabinets housed in the Victorian home's doorless alcove. She queued music on her phone and hummed through the monotonous task.

By midmorning, three empty boxes littered the foyer. She stood up to stretch her legs, find the bathroom, and get some coffee. She passed the wide staircase at the edge of the foyer and wandered further down the hall to a bathroom with a black and white-tiled floor and a clawfoot tub.

After using the bathroom, she detoured into another sitting room with high ceilings, and tall windows framed by heavy drapes. Dark beams and intricate moldings blended into the olive-green walls. A modern leather couch lived in the middle of the room, and a floor lamp beside the couch illuminated the space. Paint cans and brand-new brushes waited on a tarp in the far corner.

She walked through the outdated galley kitchen, adorned with floral wallpaper, and checked out the cabinet samples on the counter. Drew found her eyeing the cherry sample. He sighed and loosened his tie. "Hey. Thanks for the help. If you can believe it, the business is in worse shape than the remodel."

"There are some interesting colors on the walls," she murmured before she straightened and faced him. "Coffee?"

Drew poured her a mug and refilled his own. They walked back to the front of the home where Drew returned to his office —a parlor a century ago. Sun streamed through the bay window and splashed over his cherry desk, which was cluttered by his computer, phone, and more files. Penny sat on the floor of the foyer and opened another box.

At noon, Drew brought her a sandwich and told her to take a break. They sat on the wide wraparound front porch and ate their lunch. Crumbling stone steps and a rusted iron railing graced the front of the yellow Victorian home with black shutters and white trim. Penny couldn't imagine what it took to not only purchase the large home but the law practice, too. They talked about Drew's remodel and retreated to their separate tasks after lunch.

At five o'clock, Drew peeled two bills from his money clip. "I'm done for the day. Thanks for your help."

"No problem. I made progress, but there's a long way to go."

He plunked the two bills into her hand—a hundred and a twenty. She gripped the bills and shoved them into her purse. "Thanks. See ya tomorrow."

During the rest of the week, Penny sorted the boxes and bins and filed Drew's papers. On Friday at lunch, Drew poked his head out of his office. "Let's go to the CampGrounds Café for lunch. It's by the park in the center of town and has great sandwiches and coffee. My treat."

"Sounds good. I never say no to coffee."

They walked a few blocks and talked along the way. She learned that Drew had visited Misty Lake last November with a friend, who happened to be Mark's sister. Drew ate Thanksgiving dinner at Mark's house with an eclectic group of people, including an old man with a law practice and home for sale.

"I needed a break from the city and bought it cheap, but man, I've been at it for six months, and it's still a mess."

Drew held the door for Penny, and her stomach growled from the smell of yeasty sweetness. The café boasted a huge counter and six tables along a bank of windows. They sat at a table for two with their sandwiches and coffee.

"You've helped me a lot this week," said Drew. "Can you stay longer? You'd be a great assistant."

Penny stopped mid-bite of her turkey and avocado on wheat and said, "Oh, wow. Um...the job sounds great, and I love Misty Lake, but I gig for a living, and a desk job won't work for me. I need to be able to leave for performances at weird times." She put the sandwich back in her mouth and took a bite. Taste buds she didn't even know existed awakened on her tongue.

"Gigs?" asked Drew.

"I have a degree in vocal performance and sing at events like weddings and bar mitzvahs. My dream is to sing on Broadway, but I'm still in the early stages of my career." She smirked behind her sandwich. She hoped her answer sounded more professional than explaining that she sang at little kids' birthday parties because she was desperate for money.

Drew nodded. "I can be flexible. Even a little bit of help is better than the zero help I've had up to now."

"I get it, but I can't live with Mark and Emma forever."

He took a bite of his sandwich and scrunched up his nose. "I have a spare room, but I don't think Kelly would love the idea of my assistant bunking down the hall."

"Yeah. Probably not." Drew seemed like an okay guy, but living and working together was never the best idea.

The manager of the café approached their table and refilled their coffee. Drew said, "Hey, Beth. This is Penny O'Brien. She's a friend of Mark and Emma's. She's been helping me at the office this week. Do you know of any rooms for rent in Misty Lake?"

"Um . . ." Beth put her hand on her hip. "The older couple on Pine Street rent a room above their garage. It's pretty small, though."

"Want to look at it?" Drew asked Penny.

"Let me think about it over the weekend."

"Of course. If you took the job, we'd file paperwork, and I'd pay you eighteen dollars an hour."

"Sounds good. Thanks."

An older woman in a flower-print house dress and sensible shoes held onto the railings of exterior stairs leading to an apartment over a garage. Penny followed her up the metal mountain one step at a time. At the top, the woman put her hand to her chest and blew out a breath before she pulled a key out of her dress pocket and fiddled with the lock. She gave the door a shove with her shoulder and stepped inside.

A double bed hugged the wall under a window, and a worn upholstered chair sat in a corner at the foot of the bed. A kitchen sink and two-burner stove lived against one wall, and a scuffed dining table with two mismatched chairs completed the living space. Penny rounded the dining table and pushed open the door that led to a bathroom with a sink, toilet, and a shower perfect for a small child. She wasn't certain she'd be able to close the door when she sat on the toilet. The old lady twisted her hands. "We know it's cozy, but the extra money helps us with our fixed income."

The apartment couldn't be more than four hundred square feet. She didn't have a problem with the size, but giving up her gig contacts in Rochester was an issue. However, the desire to move out of her parents' house and live on her own trumped everything else. She was a college graduate—she needed to be financially independent from her parents. They earned their empty nest after four kids, and she was the last one to fly.

From the window, Penny could see the park in the center of town. A crew worked on demolishing the last of the gazebo. Two men drank coffee on a bench, a group of women chatted near the clock, and a young man walked his dog along the sidewalk. The dense wall of green in the distance soothed her soul, and the loons on the lakes called to her. She faced the old woman. "I'll take it."

Chapter Three

University of Michigan students and alumni filled the Big House to capacity the weekend after Labor Day. Beckett Young stood with his old roommates and fellow alumni in the packed stands as the world-class Michigan Marching Band played the fight song over and over again. Yet, even with the score in their favor, perfect weather, and the energy of the crowd, he couldn't get into the spirit of homecoming weekend. Grief weighed on him like a heavy, wet blanket. Despite his cousin's insistence that he had nothing to do with Helen's death, he couldn't shake the feeling he was responsible.

The Wolverines scored again, and the stadium erupted. The plan was to tailgate after the game and hit the bars at night. Beckett sank into the stadium bench. He didn't even have the stamina for the game, let alone to party all night. Just before halftime, Beckett told his buddies he wasn't feeling well. He got up and tossed his hot dog in the trash on the way out of the stadium. The crowd's roar and the drums' cadence dimmed as he walked back to his driver, who had parked three streets west of the stadium. Within the hour, Beckett was in the air.

Upon his return to Cincinnati, he sank into his couch and closed his eyes.

"Helen! Helen? Where are you? Where did you go?" Beckett screamed. Where was she? He struggled. Couldn't breathe. He needed to breathe. He needed to breathe.

Beckett gulped as he sat up on the couch. His heart pounded, bile rising in his throat. He swallowed hard and wiped the sweat from his upper lip. Darkness engulfed the living room of his condo in Cincinnati. Ugh. He'd fallen asleep and had another nightmare. Exhaustion dominated his life. He couldn't think straight.

Every time he closed his eyes, he tried to save Helen. Every. Time. A month had passed since her death, and he still couldn't figure out how to climb out of the dark hole of grief.

* * *

With a signed lease and steady job in place, Penny drove five hours to her childhood home in Rochester, Minnesota, to pack the rest of her stuff. "Mom, I'm home." Penny called to her mom from inside the front door. She tossed her coat on top of a bunch of other coats on the hooks in the foyer and kicked off her shoes.

"In here," called her mom from the kitchen. Her mom worked as a pediatric nurse at the local hospital and finished her shift by three o'clock. The first shift allowed her to be around after school for Penny and her brothers. Even though Penny and her brothers were done with school, her mom continued to work the early shift.

Macaroni noodles cooked in a pot of boiling water as Penny's mom stirred them at the stove, wearing her faded apron with her hair pulled back by a clip at the nape of her neck. Penny hugged her mom and kissed her on the cheek.

Penny's fingers brushed her mom's apron, and warm childhood memories flooded back by the dozens. Her mom had wiped tears with her apron after Penny or her brothers fell off their bikes and skinned their knees. Penny had cuddled on the couch with her mom when she was sick and pulled tissue out of the apron pocket to blow her nose. Emergency items like hair ties, rubber bands, and gum also lived in the pockets.

Penny opened the fridge, pulled out a gallon of milk, and poured a glass. She fished around the inside of a cookie jar and came up with two oatmeal raisins. She shrugged. Not her fave but good enough for a snack. She sat in her spot at the kitchen table and ate one of the cookies in two bites.

"Hungry?" asked her mom. "I made a meatloaf last night and spaghetti the night before. Leftovers are in the fridge."

"Nah. I'm good. Gonna chill before dinner." She finished her cookies and milk before she retreated to her room and flopped on her bed. Being the only girl in the family, she was blessed with her own room. Boy band posters still hung on pink walls, and trophies and ribbons cluttered her desk. Photos of her family and casts from high school musicals filled the top of her dresser. A threadbare throw rug covered the worst of the scratched hardwood.

She pulled out her phone and opened the calendar app. She had a gig at an anniversary party tomorrow at the Elks lodge at noon but wouldn't have another until two weeks after that in Duluth—a hundred miles from Misty Lake. The problem with living in Misty Lake was the travel distance to gigs. Misty Lake was about as far north as you could get before hitting the Canadian border. Drew agreed to be flexible, but her car needed to survive. Ugh. She hated dealing with her car. The oil changes and tire rotations were such a pain in the ass.

She spent the rest of the afternoon punching in numbers on her calculator. She was used to living lean, but without the safety net of her parents, the reality was bleak. An hour later, her mom let her know that dinner was ready.

Her dad, wearing his electrician's uniform with his name in cursive on the pocket, beat her to the table. Penny kissed him on the cheek and slid into her spot beside him. Her mom removed her apron and placed a bubbling tuna fish casserole, along with a green salad, on the table. After she sat down, her dad said grace. Penny waited until the ritual finished before piling a mound of food onto her plate.

"So, I've got news," said Penny.

Her dad set down his fork. He always gave her his full attention, which made her heart swell.

"I met this attorney at Mark and Emma's Labor Day party. He owns his own law practice in Misty Lake. He needed help organizing files and stuff, so I stuck around and worked for him last week. He offered me a job as his assistant. I found a cheap studio apartment over a garage, and I'm going to move to Misty Lake. Drew, the attorney, said he'd be flexible around my gigs, so it's pretty perfect."

Her dad said, "Do you have enough money for rent?"

"Yeah. It's a pretty small space, so the rent is cheap. I worked a ton of weddings this summer. And it helped to not pay rent here. Thanks."

"Do you have enough money for insurance, utilities, gas for your car, and food?" her dad asked.

"I think so," said Penny. She blew on a forkful of casserole and didn't mention the growing stack of parking tickets in her glove box. No need to worry him.

"How's your car? Are you keeping up with the maintenance?"

Penny nodded with a mouthful. She never ran out of gas. Was that regular maintenance?

"You know you can always come home if it doesn't work out, right?" said her mom.

"For sure. I love you guys, but it's time I tried this whole adulting thing on my own."

"We're so proud of you."

Armed with new sheets and a place setting for four, Penny climbed the metal staircase to her first apartment two days later. She spent the afternoon squeezing her belongings into the space. One look out of the single-pane window to the center of town and the endless forest beyond confirmed she'd made the right choice.

Money rolled into Penny's bank account as the leaves turned red, gold, and orange in the woods surrounding Misty Lake. The town's crew had completed the pergola in the park before the first snow, and Penny had attended the brief dedication ceremony. The beautiful addition featured a raised-brick area under the canopy for tables and chairs. The pergola was bigger than the old gazebo, giving the park a fresh focal point. Flowerpots would brighten the space in the spring, and Penny loved walking through it on her way to work.

Drew bought a small desk for the alcove across from his office and set Penny up with a new laptop computer. He installed a multi-line phone and painted the room a creamy white. Penny hung a few pictures to brighten the space and brought in a lamp for the desk. She answered the phone, scheduled Drew's meetings, and learned how to draft court documents.

If her math was correct, she'd be able to earn enough money by next spring to support herself while she traveled to regional show auditions. Working for Drew was satisfying, but she wanted to perform. She called the organist at the church in the center of town and told him she'd moved to Misty Lake. Remembering her from Helen's funeral, they negotiated a deal for her to sing two Sundays a month.

One Sunday morning in October, she sat in the metal chair on the altar at church and waited for the organist to finish the recessional. She waved goodbye to him and pushed out the side door into the hallway. A short, plump man dressed in tweed pants and a sport coat stopped her in the hall. He handed her a business card.

"I manage a bistro about ten miles from Misty Lake. Our diners love live entertainment, but my Friday night regular moved south for warmer weather. Your voice is beautiful and unique. Would you consider entertaining our patrons?"

Penny clasped the business card and studied it. Hmm. A regular gig could be good. Restaurants were full of different people, and diners tipped well. It was a way to get her name circulating around the area. There were brides everywhere, right? She'd also have more control over the music than she did during weddings and private parties. "I like to perform pop and folk tunes with a bit of jazz and country to keep it interesting. Would that work for you?"

"Perfect. If you're interested, come by on Friday night around seven, and sing a set. We'll talk afterwards. Can you play the piano?"

She picked her thumbnail. "Sure. Thanks. See ya Friday."

* * *

The week before Halloween, a certified letter from a law office in Misty Lake arrived at Beckett's home in Cincinnati. Beckett set his briefcase on the dining table and opened the letter before taking off his overcoat. The brief letter requested his presence at Helen's will reading the first week in January.

Another trip to Misty Lake? In the middle-of-nowhere Minnesota? He never understood why Helen loved it there, but he would honor her wishes. He reread the letter from the attorney handling the estate and marked his calendar for another trip to Misty Lake, Minnesota.

* * *

"Aargh!" Penny jumped out of her office chair as hot coffee splashed on her lap and flowed like a river across her desk. Brown stains covered a brief—she growled at her carelessness.

What a lousy end to a sucky workweek. On Wednesday, she called a family by the wrong name. She slept in on Thursday and ran into work twenty minutes late. She spent every free moment practicing the piano at the church for her gig while her work suffered.

Drew walked into her office and winced at the sight of brown stains on the brief as Penny blotted her skirt with tissue. He tossed a dead letter into her inbox—it was missing a zip code.

"Is your bistro gig tonight?" he asked.

"Yeah. I told the guy I played the piano, and I didn't lie, but I'm seriously out of practice."

"Is that why you've been so distracted all week?"

Penny nodded, heat flaring on her cheeks. She couldn't lose

her steady job. It paid the rent, and it was her ticket to getting back on stage.

"I told you when I hired you, I'd be flexible with your gigs. Fix the brief, and then go home. Come back on Monday, and start fresh."

Penny's shoulders sagged. She smiled at Drew. "Really? Thanks, boss."

"No worries. Have a good weekend."

Steam filled her studio apartment. She washed and shampooed her hair before the hot water ran out. Water droplets dripped onto her shoulders as she stood in her bra and underwear, debating what to wear.

Out of her ten polyester dresses, two of them were tight around the waist, and one had a slit up the side. Her favorite dress, a halter style with an open back, was too risqué for a restaurant gig. She settled on the conservative black dress with the scoop neckline she wore to Helen's funeral. Her long hair cascaded over her shoulders, and silver hoops dangled from her ears. She wet her thumb with her mouth and buffed a few scuffs out of her black heels.

The angled parking spaces were filled with cars and trucks in front of the bistro, but she found a space three blocks north of the restaurant. The cool weather settled her nerves as her heels clipped along the cement sidewalk at a steady beat. She pulled open the bistro's heavy wooden door, and her mouth watered from the rich smells of oregano and marinara. The man who had approached her at the church welcomed her and led her to a room with a mini fridge and a private bathroom. A couch with fluffy pillows sat along a wall, and a full-length mirror hung behind the door.

"Come out for your set at seven o'clock."

She thanked the sweet man before she hung her coat and purse on the hooks near the door. She took a moment to whirl around in a circle with her arms above her head. Her first real dressing room! It wasn't a janitor's closet or the game room at some guy's retirement party; it was her first real dressing room.

Penny checked her makeup and warmed up her voice. A soft knock sounded on the door. The manager delivered a snack of fresh fruit and hot tea. Tears sprang to her eyes, and she thanked him.

At five minutes to seven, she walked over to the shiny, black piano sitting in a corner of the restaurant. She placed her tip jar on the piano with trembling hands. She breathed deep and opened with a familiar tune. Her voice shook on the opening song, but after three pieces, she relaxed into the gig and smiled at the diners who stuffed bills into the jar.

She selected music to suit her audience of couples and families dining in the cozy restaurant, and her acapella pieces earned decent tips. When a little girl—about four years old, wearing a red dress with a big bow—walked up to her and asked for her favorite song about sunshine, Penny invited her to sit beside her as she played and sang. The little girl swung her legs on the piano bench and clapped with glee. Her parents stuffed a twenty in the tip jar. Penny gasped at their generosity and mouthed 'thank you' to the patrons.

At her break, the manager knocked on the dressing room door. "Penny, the diners love you. They want to know when you'll be back. Would you consider a regular Friday night schedule?"

Warmth flushed her body, and she clasped her hands

together to keep from hugging the old man. "I'd love to perform here on Friday nights."

The manager smiled. "Wonderful. Please enjoy a meal after your set."

After her break, a diner requested a song from a popular musical. Penny belted the tune and received roaring applause. A surge of energy burst through her, and more than anything, she wanted to be back on the stage. Soon, she promised herself. Soon.

Chapter Four

Flurries swirled around the family jet as it touched down on a slick runway in Boston just two days before Christmas. Beckett Young zipped his ski jacket and exited the plane to hug Jackson—the family driver in Boston and the man who kept watch over him during his teen years—on the tarmac. He had a smattering of gray in his beard that wasn't there the last time Beckett had been home.

"Good to see you, Mister Beckett."

"Jackson. It's been too long." He held Jackson for a moment longer, choosing not to hide his glassy eyes.

Jackson held the door of the limo while Beckett slid into the back seat and pulled a bottle of water out of the mini fridge.

Jackson circled the tarmac and glanced up at the rearview mirror with a twinkle in his eye. "How's the job?"

"HR work can be tedious, but we have an awesome basketball team at the firm. And even though I kinda suck, I get playing time."

The corners of Jackson's lips curled upward. "Seeing anyone?"

Beckett grinned. "Nah."

"You plannin' on a long visit?"

He sighed, his grin fading. The next leg of his trip filled him with dread. "Nope. I'm traveling to Minnesota the day after Christmas." Jackson nodded before allowing silence to linger between them.

Beckett relaxed against his seat while Jackson pushed his way north through thick traffic out of the city. As the sun set, the limo pulled up to a mansion on a cliff above the Atlantic Ocean, where waves crashed against the rocks. Elegant holiday decorations draped the exterior of the home and illuminated the property. House staff waited outside the front door for Beckett to exit the vehicle.

Jackson opened the limo door while the butler carried his luggage into the home. A third staff member opened the front door for him, and Beckett instinctively straightened his posture upon entering the home. He stopped in the foyer and handed his outerwear to a maid. The poor woman averted her gaze and curtsied like he was some sort of duke. He rolled his eyes at the production, wondering what fictitious infraction the maid had committed that made her act so nervous.

During college, he pushed back against the ridiculous procedures in his childhood home, but after too many arguments with his mother, he let it go and played along. Besides, he only visited once or twice a year.

Beckett wandered through a dozen rooms in the home until he found his mother in a sitting room with a tumbler of bourbon in hand. Boy, he could use one of those.

"Hey Mom, Merry Christmas."

"Don't 'hey' your mother." His mom swiped her eyes from his wavy, brown hair to his boat shoes and clicked her tongue. "I trust you've brought your tux...or a tailored suit? There's an important event tonight, and the guest list includes a senator and the state attorney general."

"I'll change, don't worry. I'll do my best not to embarrass you, Mom—Mother."

"Who is your date for this evening?"

"Solo tonight."

"Thank goodness. Several eligible women from my pre-approved courtship list will be in attendance. Please be on your best behavior, and for heaven's sake, do something with your hair."

Beckett ran his fingers through his unruly hair. He braced for the next question as his mother swallowed another sip of bourbon. "Will you stay in Boston after the holidays?"

"No. I'm headed to Minnesota, remember?" She looked at him as if he'd sprouted wings. "The will. I've been summoned to the reading of Aunt Helen's will."

His mother gazed through the window into the bleak afternoon. "It's a pity she threw her life away."

Beckett growled, "She fell in love. Her life was full in every way."

"Members of our family do not marry unskilled laborers. It was an atrocious embarrassment."

He glared at her. His mother's comment didn't dignify a response.

"Yes, well. I can't imagine what she has in her will for you. It's not like she had anything of worth."

Beckett pictured Helen's big farmhouse on the clear blue lake with the family gathered on the porch, or around the old wooden dining table, talking, laughing, or playing cards. Helen may not have had anything of great monetary value, but she had children and grandchildren who loved her. She had everything. Instead of arguing with his mother all afternoon, he said,

"I have to look in on some things for work. I'll be back down for the party."

He climbed the circular staircase to the west wing of the mansion and dumped his briefcase on the Queen Anne-style desk in the room he claimed as his own on the rare occasions he visited. He tried to work for the next few hours, but his mind drifted back to the last time he visited Helen's home on the lake, an hour north of Minneapolis. A tear fell onto his keyboard. He gave up on work and dropped onto the bed. His eyes closed a moment later.

"Helen? Helen!" His voice was silenced by the sirens screaming in the yard. "Helen! Where did you go?" The thud of footsteps on the dock pounded beside him.

A sharp knock sounded on his door. Beckett startled awake and sat up on the bed. "Mr. Young? Mr. Young, are you in there?"

Beckett shook his head from the nightmare, ambled off the bed, and opened the door to his dad's valet. He assured the man he could dress himself and sent him away. He slipped his tailored tuxedo on over his tall frame—the powder-blue bow tie complimented his eyes but pinched his throat. He took one last look in the mirror and ran his fingers through his wavy, brown hair before joining the party.

Servers walked around with appetizers, and a live band played jazz music in the ballroom. Beckett found the bar and stood in line for a beer in his own home. A woman sidled up to him, slipping her arm through his elbow.

"Beckett, you're stunning tonight."

His mother caught his gaze and nodded. Did she really

think he needed her blessing to talk to a woman at a party? He turned so his back was to his mother. "Thanks. How're you?"

"Exhausted from all the holiday parties. They have been one right after another this year."

"Uh-huh. Can I get you anything?" he asked the woman.

"No, thanks."

Beckett thanked the bartender for the beer and stepped out of line. "Where are you working these days?"

"I'm the chair for my sorority reunion. It's a thankless job."

"Oh."

Her hand found its way inside his tuxedo jacket and moved across his chest muscles until a muted growl sounded from her throat. "Why don't we go someplace and talk?"

"Uh, I'm good here."

She pouted and stood on her tiptoes to whisper in his ear. "I want to show you my recent additions."

Something hard pushed against his arm. A glance at her chest revealed cleavage plunging into her low-cut dress, but her breasts didn't squish against his suit the way they should have.

"I'm sure they're lovely, but not tonight."

He kissed her on the cheek and moved through the crowd, leaving the woman behind. Ignoring his mother's scowl, he grabbed an appetizer. After three hours and four offers—which included one from a married woman—he retreated to his room for the rest of the night.

The Christmas Eve service at the Episcopal Cathedral downtown warmed him with beautiful music and a holy message, but the façade his parents put on in front of their friends was like being in a fun house with distorting mirrors. Since he'd been home, he hadn't seen either one of his parents smile or engage the other in conversation. They didn't hold hands, and he couldn't remember if he'd ever seen them hug or kiss. Their behavior persisted over the years, and he wondered: did they ever love each other?

Christmas Day dawned. It was snowy and cold outside but frigid inside the mansion. The morning passed in silence with his mother reading and his father working on his laptop until the formal dinner at noon. Keeping with tradition, Beckett and his parents exchanged gifts at the table after the meal. He received another Rolex watch.

His mother opened the joint gift from Beckett to both of his parents. She scrunched up her nose when she pulled out the pamphlet. "Belize? You want us to go to Belize?"

"I've arranged for spa treatments and excursions. All of your meals will be prepared by a local chef in your villa."

His father coughed into his napkin. "Not sure I can get away."

His mother tossed the information aside on the table. "The Vanderbilt's went to Belize last year. She was attacked by fire ants. Can you imagine? No. We're not going there."

"But—"

"End of discussion."

Beckett tossed his napkin on the table and retreated to his room without another word. Couldn't they just say 'thank you'?

Hours later, Beckett wandered to the staff wing and found Jackson, smoking a cigar and playing cards with his buddies. A few of the housekeepers knitted, and one of the maids strummed carols on a ukulele. Laughter and conversation bubbled up from their quarters. Beckett stood outside the room, aching for a family.

"You don't have to sit in the front seat, sir," said Jackson when Beckett loaded into the car the following morning.

"May I?"

"Of course. Don't tell Mrs. Young."

Beckett winked. "Never." He fastened his seat belt beside Jackson.

"Good Christmas?" asked Jackson on the way to the airport.

Beckett shrugged. "Not really." Should he tell Jackson his parents tossed his gift aside? Again?

"Tell me about Minnesota," said Jackson.

"I'm going to a will reading for my Aunt Helen. I hope I'm able to give what she's bequeathed to me back to her family. I'm a little nervous about the weather. Misty Lake is pretty far north."

They chatted about basketball and Jackson's new lady friend. Jackson was the only thing he missed about living in Boston. When they pulled up to the family plane on the tarmac, he held Jackson in a tight hug. The man patted his back and whispered, "Call anytime."

Chapter Five

The heat in Penny's car sputtered like a confused old man. She blew on her hands at a stop light on the way to the bistro for New Year's Eve—maybe she'd take her car in after the holidays. It would be nice to drive around northern Minnesota with heat in January.

The bistro's performers split the long night, but Penny had earned the prime slot with the best tips. Once she reached the restaurant, she parked two blocks away. The nasty weather didn't stop northern Minnesota patrons from enjoying the festive night.

Tables were full, and patrons waited at the bar for an open seat. Penny warmed up in the dressing room before sauntering to the piano with her tip jar. After her opening piece, she grabbed the microphone to welcome the crowd. "It's great to see everyone on this snowy New Year's Eve. Settle in, and enjoy your delicious meal. Thanks for bein' here."

Forty minutes into her first set, a guy in jeans and a black sweater took a seat at the bar during a country song. His wavy, brown hair and chiseled cheekbones were familiar. Where did she know him from? She couldn't place him in the congregation at church. Maybe he was a client of Drew's, or maybe he attended one of Mark and Emma's parties.

While Penny crooned a love song, the guy strolled up to the piano and dropped a tip into her glass jar. He winked at her, causing her to stumble on the lyrics and hit a wrong note on the piano. It was the guy she hit with her car before Helen's funeral. What was he doing back in northern Minnesota on New Year's Eve? She regained her composure and finished the set.

Soft applause followed her last note. She said, "I'm gonna take a little break. I'll be back." She wandered over to Helen's nephew at the bar. "Hey. Thanks for the tip."

"You're welcome. Nice to see you again. You sang at my Aunt Helen's funeral," he reminded her, holding out his hand. "Beckett Young."

Her insides twisted. That sexy voice hadn't changed, and he was as stylish in jeans as he was in his expensive suit and mirrored sunglasses at Helen's funeral. "Penny O'Brien." Her hand disappeared into the heart of his palm, and a razor-sharp *zing* flew up her arm. "I also dinged your car, but we're not gonna talk about that. What're you doing back in town?"

"I'm here on business."

"Business? In Misty Lake?" Penny wrinkled her nose. "Are you selling canoes?"

His mouth lifted into his crooked smile. "It's personal."

Penny nodded. "Oh. Of course. Well, I need to get back to my dressing room before my second set. Thanks again for the tip."

"You're welcome. Happy New Year."

She retreated to the dressing room with a flutter in her chest. Wow. He was better looking than she remembered. Someone as sexy and polished as Beckett probably had a date on New Year's Eve, though. Sure enough, by the time she sat back down at the piano, Beckett Young had vanished.

* * *

Beckett clicked away from the New Year's Eve celebration on TV and lay back on the bed in the Northern Woods lodge. He threaded his fingers together behind his head and pictured Penny, serenading the patrons of the small restaurant. One of her love songs played on a continuous loop in his head. She was talented and beautiful. What was she doing in northern Minnesota?

Sleep finally came. When he woke up the following morning, he felt oddly refreshed. It wasn't until he was in the shower that he realized he hadn't had a nightmare.

* * *

The Monday morning after New Year's, Penny scurried around Drew's office setting up chairs in his conference room and brewing enough coffee for a crowd. Twenty people were due at nine in the morning for Helen's will reading. The bell over the door jingled—Penny greeted the guests and hung their coats in the closet. She checked their names off on Drew's list and directed them to the conference room. At five minutes to nine, only one attendee was missing. The name glared at her like a flashing neon sign. Her heart raced—did she have time to check her hair and makeup? A quick fluff in the reflection of her computer monitor was all she was able to accomplish before the bell jingled again. She ran her hands down her blue dress and inhaled before opening the door.

She smiled. "Mr. Young, please come in."

41

"Penny?" Beckett furrowed his brow. He turned toward the sign in the front yard and then back to the phone in his hand.

"Here for the reading of the will?" asked Penny.

Beckett nodded. "Yes."

"You're in the right place. Come on in."

Drew emerged from his office. "Is everyone here, Penny?" asked Drew.

"Yes, sir." She held out her hand to Beckett. "I'll take your coat."

Beckett thanked her and handed her his coat before following Drew into the conference room. On her way to the coat closet, she inhaled sandalwood with a hint of vanilla—or was it cinnamon? Would anyone notice if she rubbed the coat on her neck like a perfume? She laughed at herself and hung Beckett's wool coat in the closet.

Two hours later, attendees poured out of the conference room. As Penny handed each of them a packet of paperwork, a few from the group blotted their eyes with tissue, and all of them thanked her when she passed out their coats. Beckett and a middle-aged woman spoke in hushed tones. They hugged before Drew ushered Beckett back into his office.

Penny filtered through her email for the next half hour. When Drew opened his office door, she turned off the lamp in her alcove and retrieved Beckett's coat from the closet. She handed it to him.

"Thanks, Penny," said Beckett.

"No problem. I'm leavin' for lunch, boss. Can I bring you back anything from CampGrounds?"

"The usual," said Drew.

"What's CampGrounds?" asked Beckett.

"The local café," said Penny. "The manager, Beth, is a new friend of mine. She brews the best coffee in the Boundary Waters."

"Can I join you? I could use a sandwich and a good cup of coffee right about now."

Oh, geez. She didn't even wash her hair this morning and the fancy guy had asked to join her for lunch? But she said, "Sure." She shrugged into her coat and grabbed her purse. "Let's go."

* * *

Beckett's dress shoes slipped along the icy sidewalk, and he worked to maintain his balance on the way to the café. Meanwhile, Penny's red curls bounced on her shoulders as she sidestepped the ice and snow with practiced skill. Her large purse banged against her hip with each step.

"I thought you sang for a living," said Beckett.

"That's the dream, but the job with Drew pays the rent for now."

"You work two jobs?"

"Well, I work for Drew full-time and gig on the weekends. Drew is flexible with my schedule if I have a performance during the week or need extra time for travel."

He didn't know anyone who worked more than one job. Hell, he knew tons of people who didn't have to work at all. He couldn't imagine performing at night after working all day in a law office.

They turned the corner and walked around the park. Penny put her hand on his elbow and guided him around a slush puddle on the sidewalk. Her touch made his chest flutter. Once they reached the CampGrounds Café, Beckett held the door for her and breathed in a delicious mixture of sweet yeast and coffee as they walked into the warm café. He ordered a veggie panini, and Penny asked for the pastrami on rye. They both asked for coffee with three creams and one sugar.

The woman behind the counter handed over their coffees and told them she'd bring their sandwiches to their table. The tiny table for two by the window was so small, their knees bumped when they sat down. He didn't mind their closeness, but Penny slid her chair back and crossed her legs. She sipped her coffee and closed her breathtaking, green eyes to appreciate the brew. When she opened them, Beckett grinned at her.

"What?" she asked.

"You enjoy the simple things in life. It's refreshing."

Penny smirked and tilted her head. "So, Helen was your aunt, right?"

Beckett stiffened and sipped his coffee. "Aunt Helen was my dad's older sister. They were estranged."

"Oh, yeah. I remember her saying something about that."

"She married the love of her life, but her parents didn't approve. As long as she stayed married to him, she wasn't welcome around the rest of the family. I didn't get to know her until I left home. She sent me a birthday card every year, and one day in college, I called her. Helen pulled me into her circle of love at a time when I really needed it. I...I miss her."

"I'm so sorry for your loss," said Penny.

The café manager delivered their meal. Beckett wasn't sure he could get his hands around the large sandwich, but Penny dug right in. After his first bite, he wiped his mouth and sipped his coffee. He didn't want to dwell on his feelings about Helen and her death, so he said, "You sang at her funeral. How did you know her?"

"We were on the same canoe camping trip last summer." Penny peered out the window. "She taught me so much about the wilderness and life in general."

Beckett ate another bite of his panini and listened to Penny.

"As you probably know, she eloped—which is totally cool, by the way—and had a bunch of kids. She was so hip for an old lady. One hot day, after canoeing for, like, a million hours, the girls on the trip swam in a secluded cove. I wanted to skinny dip because, well, you know, skinny dipping is awesome. Helen gave me her blessing and even whipped off her top, too."

Beckett's face flushed hot—he choked on his panini and coughed until his eyes watered. The café manager brought him a glass of water. He drank and held up his hand, unbalanced from the visual of Helen skinny dipping with the tall beauty across the table. "Sorry, sorry. I'm good."

Penny smiled at him from behind her coffee mug.

He cleared his throat. "In her will, Helen tasked me with starting a nonprofit scholarship program for kids to experience the Boundary Waters."

Penny raised her eyebrows. "Cool. Creating a nonprofit sounds like something Helen would want. I bet it's a huge job."

"There isn't a timeline, but the learning curve is steep. I've hired Drew to help me with the legal logistics." Beckett sipped his coffee. Wow. The woman behind the counter brewed a mean cup of coffee.

"Have you ever done anything like this before?"

"Never. I don't know anything about the Boundary Waters."

"Sign up for a canoe camping trip. The Northern Woods' guides are great, and you'll learn a ton about the area."

Beckett's knee bounced under the table. No way. There was no way he could canoe camp in the Boundary Waters. He shook his head. "I don't think so."

She didn't pester him, so he moved the topic of conversation to favorite coffees. Penny finished every bite of her sandwich and didn't complain about the calories. She was definitely different from any other woman he'd ever met.

They finished their lunch. Penny ordered Drew's sandwich while Beckett buttoned his coat.

"I'm headed back home to Cincinnati tomorrow. Good to see you again," said Beckett.

"Thanks for lunch. See ya."

* * *

Penny waited for Drew's sandwich. She snickered when she thought back to Beckett coughing after she'd told her skinny-dipping story. It was her best Helen story; she couldn't resist sharing it with him. Beth brought over Drew's lunch and plopped down in the chair across from her.

"Who's the hottie?"

"Smokin', right? He's Helen's nephew. Remember me telling you about Helen from my camping trip? She passed last August?"

"For sure."

"Well, I keep running into Beckett. Literally. On the day of the funeral last September, I rear-ended him outside of town. He was cool about it. Now, he's back, and I've seen him at the bistro and Drew's office. He's polite and definitely hot but not my type."

"He's smitten with you."

"Nah."

"Listen, one benefit of my job is watching people for a living. I'm an expert. He likes you—he leaned in toward you, and his face glowed when you talked."

"Well, he lives in Cincinnati, and he's as polished as the chrome on a restored car. He flies home tomorrow."

"If he can escape the weather," said Beth. "A blizzard is headed our way."

Penny shrugged. "I better get back to work."

. . .

Drew sent Penny home early when the snow started to fall at dusk. She parked her car in the driveway and climbed the icy metal steps to her apartment. With a long night ahead, she decided to chat with a few college girlfriends online and stream a sitcom on her computer. Beckett jumped in and out of her thoughts throughout the evening. Beth had said he was smitten with her. Was he? The thought crossed her mind for a millisecond. No. He was too sophisticated. She realized she'd probably encounter him again, though, if Drew was his legal counsel for the new nonprofit. Hmm.

The wind howled and shook the windowpane during her dinner of ramen noodles. She tightened the loose valve on her radiator to keep it running throughout the night, but that didn't stop her from shivering in bed that night. Adulting wasn't fun every day.

Chapter Six

THE WIND WHISTLED through the night. When Beckett woke up, the snow had mounded across the Northern Woods property like whipped cream on a pie. All flights were grounded, and the roads were closed. Beckett sent a message to his boss in Cincinnati to inform him that he was stranded in northern Minnesota, though he agreed to work remotely until the airports reopened.

Another few days in Misty Lake would give him time to untangle his thoughts around Helen's request. He was humbled Helen thought he would be the best person to organize a scholarship program for kids who couldn't afford a camping trip into the Boundary Waters. He shoved aside the guilt he harbored about her death and focused on her vision.

Northern Woods was Helen's favorite place to play. When they were first getting to know one another, he asked her why she took trips to the Boundary Waters. She told him that if an individual experienced the wilderness up close, they would develop a reverence for the Earth and its inhabitants for a lifetime. Her vision with the nonprofit was to have more kids experience the wilderness, and more than anything, he wanted to honor her wishes.

Beckett showered and dressed before indulging in the buffet breakfast downstairs. Waffles, a spinach frittata, and cinnamon rolls the size of a dinner plate filled the trays. He extended his stay with the host after breakfast and retreated to his room for a full day's work.

Emails and phone calls filled his morning, but work bored him. His thoughts drifted to his lunch with Penny O'Brien. Her red hair suited her spunky personality, and his heart swelled like a balloon when she talked about Helen. He loved Penny's refreshing attitude toward life, and the image of Penny skinny dipping drove him wild—he berated himself for not getting her number.

Three days later, the airports were still closed, but the local roads had been plowed. He drove into town for a change of scenery. The bells jingled as he arrived at the CampGrounds Café. He ordered a large coffee and blueberry scone before he opened his laptop for another day of work. While he waited for his laptop to boot up, a flash of red whipped by the window. Penny O'Brien walked around the corner and pushed the café door open. He caught her eye after she ordered, and she meandered to his table.

"Still here?"

"Yep. Airports are closed. I needed a change of scenery. Care to join me?"

The manager called her order, and Penny said, "Thanks, but I'm late for work. See ya."

She grabbed her order, the bell jingling on her way out the door, and walked around the park toward Drew's office.

. . .

Beckett finished his workweek and started to generate ideas about Helen's nonprofit. Helen left a generous amount of seed money. Beckett researched how to create a nonprofit organization with an advisory board, making notes and bookmarking pages on his computer before going to bed.

On Saturday morning, a pickup truck with a plow drove across the frozen lake and pushed the snow off the ice. He ate a late breakfast in the dining hall and retreated to the lobby to read his book. A few minutes later, the lodge door opened. A rush of cold air blew in as Drew and the chef of Northern Woods entered the lodge.

"You're still in town?" Drew asked Beckett.

"Yep. Flight is rescheduled for tomorrow morning."

"This is my girlfriend, Kelly. You've been eating her food all week. We're going to skate on the lake this morning, want to join us?"

Beckett stood and shook Kelly's hand. "Your cinnamon rolls are amazing. I've enjoyed your food." To Drew he said, "Thanks, but I'll pass on skating."

The lodge's front door opened again, and his heart slammed into his chest.

* * *

Late again, Penny ran up the snowy steps and into the lobby where Drew and Kelly were talking with Beckett Young. The fancy guy again? He was everywhere. She brushed her hair off her shoulder, "Sorry, I'm late. My car had a ton of snow on it. Hey, Beckett. You're still here?" asked Penny.

"Yep. Trapped in the lodge all week."

"With reliable heat and Kelly's food—tragedy."

His low chuckle flipped her stomach.

"Wanna skate with us?" she asked. "It's pretty cold, but a few times around the ice will be fun."

"I already asked," said Drew.

Beckett shifted from foot to foot and smiled. Her face warmed. Why did he have to be so perfect? Did he ever wake up with a zit on his nose like the rest of humanity?

"Actually, I've changed my mind," said Beckett. "I could use some fresh air, and skating sounds fun. I'll join you."

"Great," said Penny. "You can rent skates from the host and meet us down by the lake."

The group dispersed. After Penny paid for her rental skates at the host stand, she pushed out the lodge door and trudged through the snow to the bench by the lakeshore. Penny tightened her laces and pulled her hat farther down on her head. She rubbed her hands together through her thin gloves and vowed to buy a warmer coat soon. Beckett sat beside her on the bench. He slipped his foot into a skate and tied the laces like one would tie a tennis shoe. *Uh oh.* Beckett might not be so perfect after all.

"You might want to pull the laces a bit tighter," said Penny.

"Tighter?"

"Have you skated before?"

"Never."

"Your ankles will be more stable if you tie the laces tight."

Beckett undid the laces and wrenched them tighter. "Oh, wow. Yeah. I can feel the difference. Thanks."

Drew and Kelly held hands, joining the group of lodge guests and local residents skating in a wide circle around the lake. Penny hopped through the snow to the cleared ice and kicked off around the loop. The cold wind stung her cheeks and burned her lungs, but the sun sparkled and bounced off the ice —it was a perfect day to skate. She skated two full laps at top speed before stopping in front of Beckett, still on the bench. Her chest heaved, and she put her hands on her hips. "You alright?"

"The lake is frozen, right? We're not gonna fall in?"

Penny laughed. "Frozen solid. No worries. Come on."

"This thin blade can't possibly hold my weight."

"I promise it will."

"There's nothing to hold onto. I'm gonna fall on my ass."

"You'll be fine. Look straight ahead, and take long strides."

"I play basketball. Is skating anything like basketball?"

"No clue. Here, hold my elbow. I'll help you get started." Penny held her elbow out to Beckett. He clutched her parka and stepped onto the ice. The man shuffled in his skates, wobbling back and forth.

"Long strides," said Penny.

"I don't think so." Beckett stopped moving his legs and balled her jacket in his fists.

"I'm not gonna pull you around the ice all day. Let's try this." Penny skated in front of him and held out both of her hands. "Hold my hands while I skate backwards."

Beckett grasped both of her hands and got his balance a bit. They skated about twenty-five feet before he bobbled again, but Penny caught him before he fell to the ice. "Look straight ahead—not at the ice."

Beckett lifted his head and stared into her eyes. Her heart skipped a beat. His blue eyes were as clear as a Boundary Waters lake, and his thick lashes were plain unfair—but she had to admit: it was amazing to be with a man who was taller than her. She'd been five foot ten since ninth grade and towered above most guys until college. Her last boyfriend even begged her not to wear heels.

Beckett's legs relaxed, and they skated the full loop around the ice. Penny pulled her hands away when Beckett appeared stable.

"Wait—don't," Beckett yelled.

"You're fine. You don't need me."

Beckett took two more strides, his arms flailing. His skates jostled into tiny steps until his feet went out from under him—he toppled backwards onto his butt. "Oomph."

Penny skated back to him and stifled a laugh. She held out her hands and helped him up from the ice.

"See. I told you I was gonna fall on my ass."

"You're doin' great." Penny held Beckett's hands over his thick gloves. Wow. They must be toasty warm. She couldn't feel her own frozen fingertips through her thin mittens.

They skated faster this time. On the second loop around, she let go of one of his hands and skated forward. Two more times around and Beckett said, "I need a break."

"Okay." Penny helped him to the bench near the edge of the lake. Still wanting to skate, she tromped back to the ice and pushed off again, leaning into her strokes to pick up speed around the loop. She twirled in the middle of the circle and skated backwards a bit before taking a break beside Beckett on the bench.

"You're good."

"My brothers played hockey growing up. We learned to skate on the homemade ice rink my dad made every winter in the backyard."

"No way—your dad built you an ice rink in your backyard?"

"Yup." She smiled at the memory. "He'd do anything for us kids. He spent hours spraying water from the garden hose in the backyard to make the rink. We'd pile onto the family room's couch every night and watch him out the back window until his gloves froze to the hose. He called us his supervisors." She snorted. "It was great for a lot of years, but when my brothers grew too big and strong, one of them smashed a hockey puck through the neighbor's window. There weren't any more backyard ice rinks after that, so we skated on the lake outside of town."

"You're lucky. Sounds like fun."

"When you grow up in Minnesota, you get creative in the winter. It's a long season."

"Why did you rent skates if you already have them?"

"My old skates are at my parents' house right now. Let's go around again."

Penny helped Beckett onto the ice, and they held hands around the circle. After two more loops, he took another break on the bench while she wove in and around people on the ice, twirling in the middle again. She did a small jump with one twist before circling around. Breathing heavy on the last lap, she admonished herself for letting her dance training lapse. Between the job with Drew and the steady gigs, she'd gotten out of shape. If she ever wanted to get back on stage, she needed to get back into regular dance training.

The group gathered by the bench. "Ready for hot chocolate in the lodge?" asked Kelly.

They hiked up the hill and retreated to the lobby, finding seats near the fireplace. They helped themselves to hot drinks at the self-serve hot chocolate and coffee station. "I'll be right back," said Kelly. She disappeared and returned with a plate of chocolate chip cookies. "My staff saved some cookies from lunch."

Penny reached for a cookie at the same time Beckett did, and they bumped hands. The spark between them caused her to flinch, and when she jerked backwards, her hot chocolate sailed into the air and down the front of her sweater.

"Oh. Damn." She dabbed the hot liquid with a napkin and

pulled her sweater away from her chest. Ugh. Wet wool was the worst.

"I'm so sorry! Hold on." Beckett set his cup down and ran from the room. Kelly retrieved a dish towel from the kitchen. The towel soaked up a lot of the liquid, but the sweater was still wet. Beckett flew back into the room and thrust a long-sleeve T-shirt and a sweatshirt at her. "Put these on. At least you'll be dry."

She hesitated, but she needed to grocery shop on the way home and didn't want to shop in a wet sweater. Alone in the bathroom, she whipped off the sodden sweater and held Beckett's dark blue, long-sleeve T-shirt up to her nose. There was his smell again—sandalwood and vanilla. The large shirt consumed her body, but she tucked it into her jeans and slipped on the sweatshirt. Warm and dry, she returned to the room. Beckett handed her a new cup of hot chocolate. "Sorry again."

"Not your fault, but thanks for the dry clothes."

The group relaxed in the comfy leather chairs and talked until Kelly excused herself to start her shift in the dining room. "I should get going too," said Penny.

Beckett tilted his head. "You're leaving?"

There was nothing she'd rather do than sit in the warm lodge, eat Kelly's cookies, and talk with Helen's nephew all afternoon, but she had a gig after her stint at the church the following day and needed to run errands. She didn't want to change back into her wet sweater and, to be honest, wouldn't mind a little more time with his scent. "How about you give me your address, and I'll ship your clothes back to you after I wash them."

Beckett typed his address and number into her phone before handing it back to her. "Keep the clothes as long as you'd like."

•   •   •

55

Lights from the park in the center of town twinkled against the night sky as Penny sat on her bed and stared out of her window. Teaching Beckett to skate was the most fun she'd had with a guy in months. She brought the hem of Beckett's sweatshirt up to her nose and closed her eyes. His smell did weird things to her belly.

She couldn't figure out why she had a crush on him. She didn't have the time to date, and he wasn't her type anyway. In the past, she'd been attracted to outdoorsy guys. Her last boyfriend drove a pickup truck and worked construction. His bulky muscles and flannel shirts made her swoon, and his thick, black hair was usually hidden under a baseball cap. They spent the fall of her senior year in college hanging out around campfires and drinking beer, but they ran out of things to talk about pretty fast. She dumped him when she caught him sexting another girl.

Beckett, on the other hand, rode in the back seat of cars driven by other people and wore expensive suits. But the way he looked at her when they had skated together twisted her gut into goo, and she didn't dare recall the sparks she felt when they held hands on the ice.

The college gear with the big block M on the front kept her warm as she scraped frost off the windowpane. She pulled out her phone and scrolled until she found his contact information. Should she text him a quick thank you? She tossed the phone back onto the bed and shook her head. He lived a thousand miles away. What were the chances she'd ever see him again?... A minute later, she picked up the phone and typed a message. She deleted it. And typed another. And then another.

So—a block M? Michigan? Her finger hovered over the device. She hit send.

A few minutes later, he typed back. *Yep. University of Michigan. Go Blue. Thanks for teaching me how to skate today.*

No problem. Let's do it again, sometime. Penny hit send and immediately cringed—she slapped her hands over her face. Yikes. Did she just ask him out? Sweat beaded her upper lip as three dots danced on her phone.

I'll be back in Misty Lake in two weeks to sign some papers for the nonprofit. I'd skate again, but would love to take you out to dinner.

Penny's pulse thrummed, and she wiped her sweaty palms on her leggings. Dinner fell into the category of an actual date. It meant getting dressed up and shaving her legs. Did she want to go on a date with Beckett? Her mind told her *no,* they were too different, it would never work, leave him alone. But her heart—and other unmentionable parts of her body—pulsed yes. Another text *pinged* while she debated her answer.

I should've asked if you're seeing anyone.

Penny typed, *Nope. No SO here.*

Great, so dinner in two weeks?

Penny bit her lip. Oh, why not? She deserved to have some fun. *Dinner works.*

Beckett replied immediately. *I'll make a reservation. See you soon.*

Chapter Seven

"She is the daughter of an Ohio state senator, I expect impeccable manners." Beckett's mother spoke to him the same way she did when he was five. He should've let the call roll over to voicemail. He never learned. She continued yammering on the line. "Do you know how hard it is to find suitable partners for you in the Midwest? I wish you'd move back home where you belong. Anyway, the driver will pick you up at six."

"Mom—I mean, Mother—I don't want to go on a blind date tonight," said Beckett.

His mother's voice ratcheted up a few notches—Beckett held the phone away from his ear. "I promised her mother you'd escort her to dinner. Her date cancelled, and she's dining with the governor's daughter. She would be an acceptable match for our family."

"You talk about this poor girl as if she's a dog with a good breeder," said Beckett. "Listen, I'm at work and can't talk. I'll go out to dinner tonight, but then I'm done. I'll find my own dates."

"You're twenty-seven years old, it's time for you to marry and father a son to carry on our name."

"Gotta go. Bye." Beckett set a reminder in his phone to pick up his tux from the dry cleaner.

* * *

Since skating last weekend, Penny had added a quick yoga practice to her morning routine to start the process of getting back in shape for dancing, but she failed to adjust her alarm and ended up rushing through breakfast. As she zipped her coat to go to work, someone knocked on her door. She squinted her eyes. No one ever walked up her icy steps. Her heart thudded. Who could it be at eight thirty in the morning on a Thursday? A peek out of the window revealed a short, bald man standing on her landing with three oversized shoe boxes at his feet.

Penny opened the door, and cold air whooshed into her apartment. She crossed her arms over her chest. "Can I help you?"

He pulled his phone out of his jacket pocket. "Penny O'Brien?"

"You found her."

"Beckett Young sent me here to fit you for a new pair of ice skates."

Penny furrowed her brow. "Excuse me?"

"I need to fit you for ice skates. Mr. Young doesn't want you skating in rental skates."

"You're kidding?"

"No."

"Well, Mr. Young doesn't get to decide what I wear on my feet. Tell him my rental skates are fine. Have a nice day."

She started to close the door, but the salesman wedged his

foot in the doorway. "Mr. Young flew me up from Minneapolis. I own a custom skate fitting business for professional figure skaters and hockey players in the cities."

She narrowed her eyes. "Impressive, but I'm still not interested. And I'm late for work." She moved to close the door again.

"Wait! Mr. Young went to a lot of trouble for you to have new skates. He chartered a private plane and hired a car and driver to bring me here. Please. I need to fit you."

Penny rolled her eyes. "No. I'll tell Beckett I sent you away. I promise you won't get in trouble. Sorry you wasted your time."

The man shrugged and headed back down the porch steps with his boxes.

She barely knew Beckett. Who was he to insist upon new skates for her? Tempted to break their date, she pulled out her phone to call him but saw the time and hustled to work. She'd call him later.

* * *

Beckett's doorman buzzed into his condo and announced the driver's arrival. Beckett straightened his tie and rode the elevator to the lobby. He slid into the back seat of the limo, and the city sped by as he rode out to the suburbs to pick up his date. His mom had emailed him a picture of the woman and her family's information. He scrolled through the details on his phone, grinding his teeth at the arrangement all the while. This is the last time, he reminded himself. *Last time.* He was done being his mother's project.

The driver pulled up to a palatial home with a circular drive and held the door for the young woman. As she slithered into the car, Beckett held out his hand. "Beckett Young. Nice to meet you."

She ignored his hand. "Yes. Well, we're dining with the governor's daughter tonight...it's a pity you're not Ivy League." She twirled her finger with a long, gel-painted nail in front of his face. "Thank God you're hot." She pulled a cigarette out of her clutch purse and put it in between her plump, lipstick-covered lips. "A light?"

"Sorry, I don't smoke," said Beckett.

She rolled her eyes. "I told my mother this wouldn't work." She stuffed the cigarette back into her purse and crossed her arms. Beckett wrinkled his nose at her caked makeup before staring out of the window. The driver pulled up to a popular downtown restaurant and held the car door open for the couple.

Soft piano music played over the hum of conversation in the restaurant. Beckett offered his arm as they weaved their way through tables. His date wore a long, silver-beaded gown with a slit up to her hip bone—her breasts pushed up and out of the bodice of her dress.

Beckett held her chair, helping her settle in, and she introduced him to the other couple. The women prattled on about ridiculous society events. Before their entrées were served, the women had drank a whole bottle of wine and ordered another. The only other man at the table answered Beckett's attempts at conversation with one-word sentences, more preoccupied with his scotch. Beckett gave up on trying to socialize, deciding to focus on his delicious prime rib. He smiled when he remembered Penny received new skates today. He couldn't wait to talk to her about it.

After dessert, they returned to the limo. His date pushed the button to raise the shield between them and the driver, then pressed her bony body against Beckett. The sour smell from the wine on her breath hit his nose. When her hand traveled up the inside of his thigh, his phone vibrated in his pocket.

* * *

After a long day at work and a box of mac 'n' cheese for dinner, Penny opened up her phone and called Beckett.

"Hmmm, you're a sexy one," a woman's voice murmured.

What the hell? She glanced at her phone, but Beckett's name flashed on the screen. Ice flowed through her veins. He wasn't alone. She slapped a hand to her forehead. Of course he was on a date, Beckett was a catch.

"Penny? I'm so glad you called," said Beckett.

"It sounds like you're on a date, so I'll make this short. Next time you want to send some guy to my door to fit me for ice skates, ask first."

"Did you like them?"

"I sent him away and told him he wouldn't be in trouble, so don't yell at him. I don't need custom ice skates." A moment of silence filled the line. The woman's soft moan echoed through the phone. Geez, this guy was too much.

"Can I call you back in a bit? I'm not in a position to talk right now."

"Yeah, I can hear you're gettin' busy. Bye."

A half hour later, Beckett's name flashed on her screen. She debated answering it, but if he was still on a date with the woman from earlier, she didn't want to talk with him. Maybe he was a girl-in-every-port kind of guy. Ugh. No thanks. Her phone rolled to voicemail, and Penny waited for the message. When it came in, she hit play and sank back into her pillows. Beckett's smooth, sexy voice filled her apartment.

"Penny. I'm sorry. As a favor to my mother, I escorted a woman to dinner with another couple. It wasn't a date, and the woman is not my girlfriend or anyone I'm interested in." Beckett paused on the message—she could hear him inhale. "I'm sorry you didn't want the skates. I bought some for myself because I signed up for lessons so you didn't have to drag me around the ice again next week. My feet didn't hurt after skating, and I thought you'd enjoy them. I should've asked you first. I hope we can still go to dinner. Have a great week."

Penny pressed play and listened to his message again. She didn't know why, but the thought of him taking skating lessons filled her with tenderness. Her irritation dissipated after listening for a third time. She saved the message.

* * *

Beckett waited two days before calling Penny. She answered on the third ring.

"I'm sorry," they both said at the same time.

"No," said Beckett. "I'm the one who has to apologize. I never should've assumed you wanted new skates. You're right. I should've asked first."

"Sorry I was harsh on the phone."

"Let's forget about it. Are we still on for skating and dinner on Saturday?"

"Sure."

Beckett breathed a sigh of relief. He wanted to get to know Penny better, and a quiet restaurant would give them the time and space to be together. She was already so different from anyone he'd ever dated. He couldn't wait to learn more about her.

Chapter Eight

The bistro was packed with diners on Friday evenings, and tips filled Penny's purse at the end of each night. Penny adjusted the microphone on top of the piano, welcoming the patrons on the frigid night. Halfway through her first set, the door opened, and a rush of cold air filled the restaurant.

Her breath caught when Beckett stomped his snow-covered shoes on the mat by the door. What was he doing here? Their date wasn't until tomorrow. He handed his overcoat to the hostess and found a seat at the bar. Women around the restaurant followed him with their eyes, and a flash of jealousy coursed through her body, but she relaxed into a love song when he waved at her. She sang to the crowd but stole glances at Beckett until the end of her first set. She made her way over to him and leaned against the bar next to his stool. Her body warmed from the closeness.

"Hey, Penny." Beckett wiped his mouth with his napkin. The gourmet burger in front of him smelled delicious, and it made her stomach rumble. He stood, giving her a quick hug and a peck on the cheek. A *zing* flew through her chest at his touch—she stumbled back a step. He caught her with his hand and held her steady. "You sound great."

"Thanks. It's easy to sing for such a nice crowd. I didn't know you were going to be here tonight."

"I flew in this morning. My meeting for the nonprofit was this afternoon, and I needed dinner. Will you have a drink with me after your set?"

"Are you sure you want to wait?"

He blinked. "Of course. I could listen to you sing all night."

"Okay. I'll see ya later." She retreated to her dressing room and leaned against the closed door. Her heart pounded, her hands vibrating from his touch. Deep breaths settled her physical response to Beckett, and she sipped her water.

A quick check of her makeup and a fluff of her hair was all she had time for before a sharp knock on the door sounded.

"Penny? You're on."

"Sorry, coming." She checked her teeth before striding out to the dining room to soft applause.

"How's everyone doin' on this snowy night? I hope my songs put you in the mood to snuggle up with a loved one." She played the intro of her next piece and entertained the patrons for another hour. She collected her tips at the end of the night before joining Beckett at the bar. He pulled out a stool for her, and she asked the bartender for a soda and a plate of ravioli.

"So, skating lessons?" Penny asked while they waited for her meal.

"My skating teacher told me I made a lot of progress last week. The lessons are every other day before the hockey teams take over the ice. With luck, you won't have to drag me around the ice tomorrow."

The bartender placed Penny's ravioli in front of her, and she inhaled the steaming marinara. "Private skating lessons?"

"Well, I could've joined the three- to five-year-olds at

eleven o'clock in the morning on Tuesdays, but it kinda conflicted with work."

Penny nodded. "Where do you work?" She blew on a bite of her ravioli and wrapped her lips around the fork.

"I'm an employee relations specialist for a large PR company in Cincinnati. Basically, I help orient new employees to the policies and procedures of the firm."

"Sounds interesting."

Beckett shrugged. "It's not bad. I meet a lot of people."

They talked until the servers turned the chairs upside down on the tables. Beckett followed her to the dressing room and helped her with her coat. After she collected her purse, they walked to their cars in the dark night.

"Thanks for coming tonight. I'll drive over to Northern Woods at ten tomorrow. Sound good?" said Penny.

"Perfect." He held her door, and she slid into her seat. She turned the key in the ignition, but nothing happened.

"C'mon, c'mon." She tried again, and the engine sputtered but died before it turned over.

Beckett yelled through the window. "What's going on?"

She rolled down her window with the hand crank and said, "She doesn't like the cold. Don't worry, she always starts for me. You don't have to wait." The window squeaked on the way back up. Geez—how embarrassing. She patted the dashboard. "C'mon darlin, don't fail me in front of the stylish guy." One more turn of the key and the car coughed and sputtered before roaring to life. Penny waved to Beckett as she pulled out of the space.

* * *

Beckett woke up to sun streaming through the window in his room at the Northern Woods lodge. He wasn't sweaty, and his heart beat a normal rhythm. He lay flat on his back and laced his fingers behind his head. He smiled. No nightmare.

What would Helen think about his attraction to Penny O'Brien? Oh, how he wished she were here to ask.

After a long shower and big breakfast of stuffed french toast and sausage, he zipped his ski jacket and collected his skates, hat, and gloves to wait for Penny downstairs. By ten after ten, he began to pace the lobby. At ten fifteen, he texted her but didn't get a response. The door flew open at ten twenty, and she ran into the lobby.

"Sorry, I'm late," said Penny. "I talked to my mom on the phone this morning and lost track of time. She was telling me all about my niece's dance recital and droned on and on about the costume."

"No worries. Glad you made it."

After she rented her skates, she said, "Ready?"

"Let's go." They walked down to the shore of the frozen lake and sat on a bench to change out of their boots and into skates.

Penny eyed his new lightweight skates with thick padding and sharp blades. He shrugged. "I need all the help I can get."

Beckett's eyes adjusted to the glare of the sun bouncing off the ice. Once laced, Penny stepped onto the frozen lake first. Beckett joined her. After a minute of bobbling, he strode around the loop. Penny laughed and clapped her hands from the other side of the circle. She cupped her hands around her mouth, "You're doing great."

"It's harder than it looks," he shouted back to her.

She glided up to him, and they skated side by side. "It takes guts to learn how to skate as an adult."

He blushed. "Thanks."

She grabbed his hand, and he squeezed it, thrilled with her spontaneity. He didn't want to let go of her hand for the rest of the morning, but his legs burned in protest from the strain of staying upright on superthin blades.

When he didn't think he could manage another minute on the ice, he let go of her hand and sat on the bench. He stretched out his legs while Penny twirled in the center of the circle—she spun so fast she was a blur. She burst with confidence, and Beckett couldn't take his eyes off her. He loved her attitude. Other guys on the ice stole looks at her, too.

After his legs recovered, he bobbled back onto the ice. Penny slowed beside him, and he grabbed her hand again. She grinned at him, matching his stride. When their cheeks were red and their fingers frozen, they retreated to the bench to remove their skates. He turned toward Penny as she tugged on her boots. When she finished, they stared at one another. Her emerald eyes sparkled, and her smile filled her face. The urge to kiss her blasted through his body. He leaned down to her lips —but she turned her head, and he got a mouthful of curly hair. She hopped off the bench, and he followed her up the hill.

Chapter Nine

Music blared in Penny's apartment. She sang along as she pulled on tights for her date. It had been a long, long time since a guy took her out on a proper date. Singing at the bistro sometimes made her feel like she was the only person on the planet not in a relationship. On Friday nights, the restaurant was filled with lovey-dovey couples who held hands over their meal and played footsie under the table. She'd even caught a few couples kissing and hurrying to pay their bill.

Standing in front of her closet, she stared at her ten dresses. She slipped into her maroon dress with the keyhole neckline and shoved her feet into black dress boots. Her usual silver hoops and plain silver necklace completed her outfit. The parka ruined her look, but it was her only coat, and January in Misty Lake was always below freezing.

When car lights swooped into the driveway downstairs, she killed the music, stepped out of her apartment, and locked the door. Beckett met her halfway up the snowy stairs and offered a gloved hand.

"I would've come to your door."

She accepted his hand. "It's okay. I'm a big girl."

He opened the car door, and Penny slipped inside.

Beckett slid into the driver's seat, and the outside noises silenced when the door closed. He pushed a button to start the car—he didn't even use a key.

They drove around the park, but she couldn't hear the engine. Jazz music piped into the cabin, and the leather seat warmed under her dress. Wow. "This is a pretty nice car."

Beckett shrugged. "It's a rental. Speaking of cars, what's going on with yours?"

"It's the car my brothers and I shared in high school. It's super old and even has a crank handle for the window, but it works. I bought it from my parents after college. She's all mine, but she doesn't like the cold. Sometimes she needs a little sweet talking to get her going."

"It's frigid up here. What if you break down?"

"I know how to do some stuff. My dad taught us all how to change a tire and jump the battery. I'll be fine."

"When you're ready to buy a new one, I can help you look. It's fun to test drive new cars."

She snorted. "I bet." This guy had no idea how different they were.

Beckett glanced at her and merged onto the highway. "If you're an aunt, you must have a brother or a sister."

"Three older brothers. Two of them are married with kids."

"Holidays must be fun."

"More like organized chaos. How many sibs do you have?"

"I'm an only child, and I grew up north of Boston. My dad's a judge. My mom manages the house and staff."

"Staff?"

"Yeah. You know—butlers, maids, cooks, drivers, gardeners."

Penny turned toward him in the seat. "You're serious? Do they live there?"

"Um...yeah. I mean, they have their own wing in the house."

Silence stretched between them as she contemplated the size of a house requiring a live-in staff to maintain it.

"What do your parents do?" Beckett asked her a few moments later.

"My mom's a nurse, and my dad's an electrician." She waited a moment. "No staff." Laughter filled the car. "How's the nonprofit going?"

"There're a lot of legal logistics. Drew has been helpful, but we still need a name."

"Ooh, a name." She tapped her chin with her finger.

"If you have any ideas, throw them my way."

"I'll think about it."

They rode in silence for a few miles. "You should host a fundraiser for the charity," Penny started, "as an introduction to your mission. You could charge per seat or per table and serve some fantastic food."

"That's a great idea," said Beckett. "There should be music, too."

"Dancing," said Penny. "Call it a gala, and people will swarm to the event."

"Would you be willing to entertain the crowd?"

"During dinner, yes, but you should hire a band or DJ for the dancing portion of the evening."

"I'll make a note of it. Of course, the board would have to approve everything."

More silence filled the car. Penny didn't want to distract Beckett too much during the forty-mile drive along dark, snowy roads.

When they arrived at the restaurant, Beckett hopped out of

the car and opened her door. Her surprise must have shown on her face because he said, "What?"

"I've seen guys open doors on TV and in the movies, but this is the first time it's ever happened to me."

"I'm glad I was your first." Beckett held out a gloved hand. When she accepted it, an electric arc snapped to life between them again—they paused while their eyes connected. If it wasn't for the wind and cold, she would've stared into his eyes all night in the dark parking lot.

Beckett shut the car door and held her hand all the way into the restaurant. The host took their coats before Beckett led Penny to their table with his hand on her lower back. He pulled out her chair, and she sat on the cushioned leather seat.

"Do you like wine?" asked Beckett.

"Sure. My roommate in college always had a box of wine in the fridge. One day, we were out of milk, and she shrugged her shoulders and held her cereal bowl under the spout."

Beckett laughed and waved a server to their table. He ordered something in French, and within a few minutes, the server returned with a bottle of wine and went through a big production before she poured two glasses and set the bottle on their table.

Relieved that Beckett handled the wine, Penny leaned across the table. "Do people ever send the bottle away if they don't like the taste? And what if it's awful? Do they spit it out? Where?"

Beckett's double dimple made another appearance. "It's a silly production, but the bottle is from a good year."

She sipped the wine, and the smooth liquid coated her throat. "Oh, wow. That's good. Way better than box wine."

A different server announced their specials and handed them leather-bound menus the size of a briefcase. Penny was starting to relax until she opened the menu. She muffled a gasp, and snapped it closed. Beckett peered over his menu. "Penny?"

Penny leaned across the table and whispered, "This place is too expensive. Who pays twenty bucks for an appetizer?" She reopened her menu but couldn't find an entrée for less than forty dollars. She set the menu on the table—she didn't think she could eat.

Beckett closed his menu and placed his hand on top of hers. The warmth of his hand slowed her heart rate—she exhaled. He said, "I've got this. Please. I'd like to buy you dinner." After he pulled his hand away, she reopened her menu a third time. "See anything you like?" said Beckett.

"The pasta and the short ribs look good." She didn't tell him she didn't recognize a lot of the other food on the menu.

"I'm going to order the duck."

Penny ordered the short ribs and sighed when the server removed the menu with the expensive prices out of her hands. She sipped her wine and scanned the restaurant. Candlelight and flowers decorated every table. Art covered the walls, and musicians had set up in the corner behind the dance floor.

"I hope the music starts soon," said Penny.

"The reviews raved about the music. Would you ever perform here?"

"I bet the tips are awesome, but it's a long drive in the winter."

Their appetizer arrived. Penny picked up a crostini and bit off a small piece. She moaned. "Delicious."

Beckett smiled. The band started to play, and Penny tapped her foot to the beat under the table. Her short ribs and creamy mashed potatoes melted in her mouth. Beckett offered her a bite of his duck—the strong flavor and tenderness of the meat surprised her, but she liked it. When the server removed their plates, Beckett held out his hand. "Will you dance with me?"

She smiled at him. "Of course. I love to dance. Fourteen years of dance lessons. Watch out."

Penny accepted his hand. He led her out to the dance floor without breaking eye contact and twirled her around. Wow—this guy could dance. The men she usually dated swayed back and forth like they were at a high school prom.

The music moved to a piece in 3/4 time, and Beckett flawlessly transitioned into a waltz. Penny followed his lead and said, "Where did you learn how to dance?"

"My mother signed me up for ballroom dance lessons in eighth grade. All the girls were taller than me, and I stepped on their feet. I lacked any sense of rhythm and bumped into other kids on the dance floor. My mother was so horrified, she pulled me from the class and hired a private teacher to come to the house." Beckett's cheeks turned a light shade of pink. "My dance teacher was the prettiest lady I'd ever seen in all my thirteen years, and I developed a huge crush on her. She taught me to feel the beat."

"She did a great job."

A slow love song brought them closer together on the dance floor. Her legs brushed against his thighs, and her chest swiped his suit jacket. He moved her hair off her shoulder and whispered in her ear, "You're stunning." She shivered from his warm breath on her neck and pressed closer to him.

When the dance ended, he led her back to their table for dessert. They split a chocolate ganache cake and sipped their coffee. Beckett paid their bill before helping Penny with her coat. The long car ride back to Misty Lake gave them more time to talk. Beckett had helped Penny out of her comfort zone in the expensive restaurant with food she didn't recognize. Once they reached her driveway, she turned to face him. "Thanks. I had a great time."

"So did I." He opened her door and held out a gloved hand.

She grasped his hand and stepped out of the warm car, wind whipping around them. Although her heels sank into the frozen slush on the driveway, Beckett's gaze scorched her body from head to toe. Beckett squeezed her hand and leaned down to her face. His lips slid against hers, and they locked into a perfect union. A kaleidoscope of colors exploded behind her closed eyes—she trembled. Beckett released her lips. "You're cold. You should get inside."

Penny shook her head. "Not cold." She balanced on her tiptoes, tilted her face up toward his and kissed him back. Her fist clenched around the lapel of his wool coat, and he rested a hand on her hip.

Beckett broke the kiss and leaned his forehead against hers. "Can I see you again?"

Her body screamed yes—she couldn't remember ever feeling such a rush of passion after a first kiss, but her brain wasn't so sure. Doubt slammed into her gut. He lived so far away. She'd never had a long-distance relationship. How did it work? And Misty Lake was temporary for her—what would happen when she returned to the stage? Would a relationship survive a career on the road?

She did need a date for Mark and Emma's wedding, though. One more date couldn't hurt, could it? Penny screwed up her courage and said, "My friends, Mark and Emma, are getting married in two weeks at Northern Woods. Will you be my plus one?"

Beckett's face broke into a big smile. "Love to."

After one more tantalizing kiss, she whispered goodbye and scurried up her steps.

. . .

Penny peeked out of her frost-covered window, watching the taillights of Beckett's car disappear around the park and back to Northern Woods. Her body vibrated—she longed to feel his lips against hers again. The first date fueled desire. She stripped off her dress and dug around in her closet until she found his Michigan T-shirt. As soon as she slipped it on over her head, the faint sandalwood and vanilla scent brought a smile to her face. She curled under the sheets on the frosty night.

Beckett had opened her car door and ordered wine in French. He could ballroom dance and had parents who employed 'staff' in their home. He definitely played on a different level, but their connection filled her with a longing she'd never experienced with any other guy.

They danced on a cloud. Penny's long, red hair tickled his chin. Her dress swished as he spun her around, and her smile reached her eyes. The musicians played love song after love song, and the night never turned to morning. They danced and kissed until he swept her up into his arms and carried her off the cloud.

Sweat covered his body as he startled awake in his bed at Northern Woods. He panted through his fast pulse and placed a hand on his chest to slow his breathing. But the dream—it wasn't a nightmare. Penny in his arms and dancing on a cloud was definitely not a nightmare. He lay back down in bed with a smile. He closed his eyes and continued the dream.

Chapter Ten

Midday, the Monday after her date with Beckett, Penny called to Drew from the door of the office on her way out, "I'm running over to Emma's for lunch." Drew waved her off.

Penny hopped into her car for the short ride to Emma's house. She parked in the lot and searched the store for Emma.

"Emma around?" she asked Mark.

"She's finalizing the wedding menu with Kelly. They're in the house."

"Great. Thanks." She walked the path to their home, knocked, and called for Emma from the front door.

"Penny?" asked Emma. "Is that you? Come on in."

Penny kept her coat on and joined Emma and Kelly at the dining table. Spreadsheets and lists covered the table between the women, and Kelly typed on a laptop computer.

"Hi. Sorry to interrupt. Emma, can I change my RSVP from one to two? I'd like to bring a date."

Emma lifted her head from the mess of papers and grinned at her. "A date?"

Penny stuffed her hands in her coat pockets and blushed.

"Yeah. Will it screw up your seating charts? Because we can pull a chair up to the table and squeeze him in."

Emma waved her hand at Penny. "I'll fit him in, just don't tell my mother."

Penny smiled. "Got it."

"Are you bringing Beckett?" asked Kelly.

"Who's Beckett?" asked Emma. "And I'll need a full name for the seating chart."

"Beckett Young. He's Helen's nephew—I met him at the funeral. Drew is helping him get a nonprofit started."

"He's dreamy," said Kelly. "He spent a week at Northern Woods during the blizzard and stayed again this past weekend."

Penny smiled. "Yeah. We went out to dinner on Saturday night."

"Ooh. Well, sit down, girl, and give us some details," said Kelly.

"I've got to get back to work, but I'll fill you in at the bachelorette party," said Penny.

Kelly winked at her, and Emma jotted a note on a different piece of paper. "All set," said Emma. "You're still singing, right?"

"For sure," said Penny.

"Don't be late," said Emma.

"Never." She hugged Emma and waved goodbye to Kelly.

Two weeks later, Penny grimaced as the tequila shot scorched the back of her throat. She set the shot glass onto Emma's coffee table. "I need to sing at the wedding tomorrow. I'm done." Emma handed Penny a water bottle.

"Not me," said Beth as she poured another shot of tequila.

Emma and Kelly giggled.

"Open your gifts, Emma," said Penny. The women sat around Emma's great room after dinner with a bottle of wine and tequila.

Penny shoved the wrapped gifts across the couch to Emma. By the time she finished opening the boxes, lingerie was scattered across the room. Penny held up a teddy while Beth admired a chemise, and Emma chuckled at the pile of colorful thongs. Kelly poured more wine into her glass and said, "You're so lucky, Emma, I can't wait to be married."

Beth screwed up her nose. "Anything beyond a hook-up is too much for me."

"You're young. I'm gonna be thirty soon," said Kelly.

"I think it depends on the person," said Emma.

"How do you even know if the person you're dating is the one?" asked Penny.

"When the right person comes along, you'll know. It feels like home," said Emma.

"But there're so many different feelings. Passion, infatuation, lust, love. How do you know when you're in love?" asked Penny.

Kelly swooned. "Ooh, love. Love makes you all tingly and warm."

"Nah, that's lust," Beth grunted. "I'd settle for lust. I haven't had sex in three months."

Penny tucked her feet under her legs on the couch. "I think I like Beckett...a lot." Did she really say that out loud?

Beth fanned herself. "He's a hottie."

"Tell us about your date," said Emma.

"He came into town on Friday and ate a burger at the bistro while I performed. We skated the next morning and went out to dinner."

"And?" said Beth.

"He drove me home." She surveyed the room. "We kissed."

"And?" said Kelly.

"Just a kiss, but . . ." She picked her fingernail. "I wanted more. A lot more. I've...waited."

"Waited? Waited for what?" said Beth.

"Sex. I wanted to wait for love," said Penny.

Silence filled the room until Kelly said, "Are you serious?"

Penny sipped from her water bottle and nodded. "I'm still waiting."

Beth shook her head and waved a finger at Penny. "You have way more self-control than me."

"I've never dated anyone where sex even crossed my mind, and I'm already thinking about it with Beckett after one kiss," said Penny.

Emma patted her knee. "Follow your heart. You'll know when it's right for you."

The next afternoon, Penny received a *help me—get my mother out of here* text from Emma. She snickered as she rode the Northern Woods elevator to the top floor and entered the bridal suite. "Mrs. Richards, the florist forgot the cake topper," said Penny. "She really needs your help downstairs."

Emma's mother gasped—she shook her finger at her daughter. "This is why you don't get married in the middle of nowhere." Emma's mom left the suite in a huff.

Emma, dressed in a cream-colored sheath with a flower in her hair, breathed out a long sigh and turned to Penny. "Thanks."

"No sweat. You look gorgeous. I'm early. Mark is dressed and waiting, and Kelly's cake is beautiful. See you downstairs."

Penny swung her purse over her shoulder and left Emma's suite to warm up her voice in the conference room. She punched the lobby button on the elevator, but it stopped on the second floor. When the doors swished open, Beckett stood on the threshold. He smiled when their eyes met, and he walked into the elevator.

"Hey," Beckett's smooth voice crooned to her.

"Thanks for coming," she said. She stole a look at him as he brushed a hand through his hair. He wore a dark gray suit with a lavender polka-dot tie. His dress shoes were brand new. Her old black dress—the same one she wore to Helen's funeral—and her dress boots had seen better days. His polished look seemed effortless, whereas she'd spent the morning buffing out the worst of the scuffs on her boots with Vaseline. The elevator opened up to the lobby, where Penny and Beckett exited and stepped to the side. "Are you nervous?" asked Beckett.

Penny forgot all about her outfit. "Nah. Weddings are easy, but I have to warm up my voice before the service."

"You're singing the prelude and, again, during the lighting of the unity candle, right?"

Her chest fluttered. He remembered her singing schedule from when they talked about the wedding late last week. "Yeah."

"Great. I'll see you after the ceremony." He reached for her hand and squeezed it. "See you in a little while."

Penny floated to the conference room and warmed up her voice.

* * *

Beckett sat with Drew, waiting as the other wedding guests were seated. Penny walked in from a side door and nodded to a pianist. Beckett couldn't peel his eyes from her. She'd put her hair up in some sort of knot, and it left her neck bare. Had he ever seen anything so sexy? He loved her height and couldn't wait to dance with her at the reception.

Her music quieted the crowd. Goosebumps broke out on his arms from the timbre of her voice. He didn't know what it took to land a part in a show on the stage, but he couldn't imagine anyone with a more sensual voice. How did she find the nerve to sing in front of people? She caught his eye near the end of her piece and didn't look away until the last note faded.

A message of love and patience preceded the vows and rings. Penny stood up again for the lighting of the unity candle. Her love song brought tears to the bride's eyes. The newlyweds filed down the aisle and greeted their guests in a reception line. Beckett waited for Penny at his seat, and when the pianist finished the recessional, she joined him. He stood and clasped both of her hands in his. "You were fantastic. I love listening to you sing." He kissed her on the cheek.

"Aww, thanks. Weddings are fun. I do a lot of them. Last year I sang in seventeen weddings. It's easy money and free entertainment. Weddings are full of drama. You'd never believe some of the things I've seen and heard."

He chuckled. "I bet."

Penny looped her arm through his and introduced him to the bride and groom in the receiving line. Afterwards, she guided him to their table in the Northern Woods dining hall, decorated for the wedding. They were seated with Drew and a few of Emma's friends from Chicago. Kelly worked in the kitchen with the food and promised to join them for dancing later. The group introduced themselves and made small talk through the roast beef dinner. Penny excused herself to use the bathroom after the dancing started, and one of the women from Chicago slid into her empty chair.

"So, you're from Cincinnati?" the woman asked Beckett while twirling her hair with her fingers.

He nodded. "From Boston originally, but I live and work in Cincinnati now."

She picked an imaginary piece of lint off his suit lapel. Her finger lingered longer than it should have. "You must be a doctor? Lawyer?"

He shifted in his seat and scanned the room for Penny. Where was she? Why did women always take forever in the bathroom? "Um, no. I work for a PR firm."

"Ooh, you must know a lot of famous people." She crossed her leg, and her dress hiked up her thigh. The lacy top of her stocking peeked out from the hem of her dress. Beckett scooted his chair back and searched for Penny again.

"Not really. My job is in HR."

The woman shifted and rubbed her high heel against his calf. She smiled at him. "Will you dance with me?"

He looked from the woman to the door again, but Penny didn't appear. One dance wouldn't hurt. He'd be able to hold her at arm's length. If they stayed at the table, she'd maneuver her way onto his lap. "Sure."

They stepped onto the dance floor, and she draped her body over him, but he clasped her hands and held them in the correct positions. He led her around the dance floor while she yammered on about their harrowing flight from Chicago to Minnesota. He made a comment the woman must have thought was funny because she laughed and tossed her head back before pressing her body against him. They turned on the dance floor and—Penny stood at their table with her arms crossed and her lips pursed together. He mouthed to her, "Help me," but she whipped back around and disappeared.

* * *

Penny burst through the bathroom door in the Northern Woods lobby and placed two hands on the sink. Beth was splashing water onto her face at the sink next to her.

Beth patted her mottled cheeks with a paper towel and glanced at Penny. "Whoa, what's wrong?"

"I leave for two minutes," Penny fumed, "and he's got a gorgeous woman plastered all over his thousand-dollar suit on the dance floor. This isn't gonna work. He's too much of a playboy for me. What was I thinking?" Penny's shouts echoed off the tiled bathroom wall.

Beth closed her eyes and held her hand up to Penny's face. "First of all, shh." She put her hand down. "Second, maybe the woman dragged him onto the dance floor. Beckett seems like a nice guy who would dance with a woman to be polite. Go back to the table and talk with him. First rule in relationships is to never assume. I should know, I break it every damn time."

Penny paced the small space. "I was so stupid to think someone like Beckett would be interested in me. That tall blond from Chicago is closer to his age, with a career and designer clothes and everything. I bet she doesn't use Vaseline on her scuffed boots."

Beth grabbed her arm. "Stop. Go talk with him." Beth leaned over the sink again. "Seriously? How're you not as hungover as me?"

"I stopped drinking when you started the shots. Alcohol kills my voice."

"Ugh." Beth held her head.

"Sorry." Penny rubbed Beth's back. "Feel better."

She left Beth in the bathroom and returned to the dining hall. Beckett and the woman were back at the table—she had her hand on his thigh as he scanned the room. He jumped up when Penny approached. "The DJ announced sleigh rides around the property. Let's go," said Beckett.

"Um, sure." He grabbed her hand and led the way. She jogged to keep up with him.

They bundled into their coats and gloves and waited on the porch for the sleigh.

When it was their turn, they loaded into the horse-drawn sleigh, and Beckett covered them with a blanket and said, "Why didn't you save me on the dance floor?"

She turned to him with wide eyes. "You seemed pretty comfortable."

"She asked me to dance. Being polite, I accepted, but she turned handsy pretty fast."

"You're not interested in her?"

Beckett snorted. "Not in the least."

Penny snuggled closer to Beckett on the bench seat. "Really?"

"Really. If you need to hit the bathroom again, give me a heads up."

Beth was right. He had danced with the woman to be polite. She slipped her hand under the blanket, and they threaded their fingers together. When the sleigh turned toward the woods, Beckett captured her chilly lips in a kiss until a bump knocked them apart. He ran his thumb along her knuckles under the blanket until they returned to the Northern Woods porch.

"Dance with me?" he asked.

Penny nodded.

They hung up their coats before Beckett led her to the dance floor. Their bodies pressed together, and they danced the rest of the night. Penny pretended not to notice the scowl on the other woman's face, but her inner cheerleader jumped for joy.

Beckett walked Penny to her car at the end of the night. He angled her against the driver's side door and enveloped her in a deep kiss. After being with people the whole night, she relished the darkness and alone time with him. She brushed her tongue against his lips, and he opened for her. His velvety tongue glided along hers—the new sensations deepened in their embrace while Beckett pressed himself against the v of her thighs.

Beckett breathed and kissed the sides of her lips. "I don't want to leave," he said.

"But you have a basketball game in the morning, right? And I have to sing at the church tomorrow. How did you get a flight this late at night, anyway?"

"It wasn't a problem." He kissed her neck, and she tilted her head away from him to expose more skin. His hands cupped her cheeks—their lips met again. The wind howled, and they pulled apart.

"Thanks for being my plus one," said Penny. "I forgot to bring your T-shirt and sweatshirt."

"Keep them. I have too many."

"Really? I love sleeping in your T-shirt."

Beckett groaned against her lips and kissed her again. "What're you doing for Valentine's Day?"

"The Misty Lake Love Snow Festival is Valentine's weekend. I'm performing for part of the weekend. I'm told it's a fun event."

"We'll talk."

"Okay."

Beckett held her face and kissed her until her knees turned to taffy, like the kind her dad used to buy her at the fair. After they parted, she got in her car and leaned her forehead against her steering wheel, catching her breath. Seven years of dating did *not* prepare her for this. Yikes. Her body liquified every time Beckett kissed her.

The short drive back home didn't do anything to cool her longing. She flung her parka on the chair and stripped out of her dress to put on flannel pajama bottoms and Beckett's T-shirt. She found her fleece socks under the bed and shoved them onto her frozen toes.

Replaying the night filled with dancing, a sleigh ride, and more kisses in the freezing cold made her want to fuse her body with his and never part. She'd kissed a lot of guys in high school and college, but Beckett's kisses sent her flying. Her phone *binged* with a text. *I had a great time at the wedding. I can't wait to see you again.*

The endorphins gushed all over again. She typed back, *So did I. You're fun to kiss.*

Beckett replied, *Same*, with kissing emojis.

Chapter Eleven

Another basketball swished through the net, and Beckett ran down the court. He was on tonight—a rare occurrence for him. Sweat poured down his head. A teammate stole the ball and passed it to Beckett, who came open in the corner. He hit a three as the buzzer sounded—they won the game.

"Young, you scored tonight," smirked his best friend and officemate. "You buying the beers?"

Beckett laughed. "I always buy the beers." The team hit the locker room and, afterwards, met at the bar around the corner for dinner and drinks. The guys ate burgers and wings. When their plates were decimated, most of them went home to their wives and families, but Beckett and his buddy hung around for one more beer.

"Okay. What's going on?" asked his best friend. They had started HR jobs at the company together six years ago and became fast friends. Beckett worked in employee relations, and his friend worked in benefits. A native Ohioan and a graduate of Ohio State University, he provided Beckett with a fierce rivalry during football season. They hung with the same group of guys and played basketball together after work and on the weekends. "You're hittin' threes and smiling for the first time since summer."

Beckett ran a hand through his still-damp hair. Smiling for the first time since summer? He was probably right. Penny had definitely distracted him from the grief since January. "I met a woman."

"Another setup?"

Beckett growled. "No. Penny lives in Misty Lake. She's an assistant to the attorney who is helping with the nonprofit stuff."

"So, definitely not from your parents' 'approved list.'"

Beckett snorted. "No."

"Mommy will go ballistic."

"Probably." Beckett took a long pull from his beer and dismissed any thoughts of his parents. "But nothing's too serious, yet."

"It never is with you."

Beckett frowned at his friend's accurate description. Usually, he went out with a woman once or twice before they had sex. Then they dated for a few weeks before breaking up because of some trivial excuse, like Beckett hating her perfume or being unable to handle her obsession with ax throwing.

His last girlfriend worked in the accounting division at the office two floors below him. She flirted with him during staff meetings, and he created excuses to visit her floor. She invited him to trivia night at a local bar. They had fun for a couple of weeks, but she turned serious once he invited her up to his condo and flew her to Florida for a weekend.

It was the longest he'd ever dated anyone, but when she broached the subject of living together and peppered him with questions about his money and his family, he broke up with her. He claimed he could never be in a long-term relationship with someone who rooted for the SEC. She had graduated from the University of Florida and was a diehard Gator fan. She pouted and begged him to reconsider, but he didn't budge.

Dating casually had always been his go-to plan to avoid anything serious that would involve meeting his parents or disclosing the details surrounding his family trust. As a result, he not only irritated his mother, but he also never experienced a serious, steady relationship. Now, Penny already had him shoving aside his anxiety and diving straight into the deep end of the relationship pool.

Beckett tossed enough cash on the bar to cover the tab and a generous tip for the bartender. "I'll see you tomorrow."

His best friend grabbed his elbow and said, "Really—it's great to see you back to normal."

Beckett nodded and walked the long way home. Up until he met Penny, he lived in a closed box with stale air. Penny opened the box and let all the fresh air inside, offering him a new perspective on life.

* * *

On Thursday night, Penny serenaded the donors during the dinner portion of the fundraiser for continued clean water in the Boundary Waters. The snowy drive to St. Paul tested Penny's patience, but she arrived only twenty minutes late. Soft music selections and jazz piano filled her set, enabling diners to talk during their meal. Once the remarks and slideshow began, Penny ate her chicken and broccolini in the kitchen with the servers before heading home.

When she emerged from the venue, an inch of snow layered her windshield. She rummaged around in her back seat for the scraper. "Why do I live in Minnesota?" she grumbled to herself. Her car protested in the cold, but eventually started up.

She drove for an hour until her car bumped and pulled to the right. "Shit." She maneuvered to the side of the highway, got out, and shined her phone flashlight on her flat rear tire. Ugh.

Her dad taught her how to change a tire years ago. There were two things she needed: a jack and a spare. She doubted the old car had either, but a quick look in the trunk confirmed both. She climbed back into the car. After warming her fingers against the vents, she rustled around in the glove box for the manual with the step-by-step directions to refresh her memory of the procedure. Her phone rang. Beckett's name flashed on the screen.

"Hey, Beckett."

"Can you talk?"

"Sure. After I change my flat."

Beckett's voice sharpened, "Where are you? It's almost nine."

"Oh, I'm, like, an hour outside of St. Paul. I had a gig tonight in the city. My tire blew. My dad taught me how to change a flat, and I've got the manual if I get stuck. I'm good."

"When I have car trouble, I call the auto club. How about I call them for you?"

Penny shoved her parking tickets aside in the glove box and dug out the manual. "Thanks, but I know how to read directions, and I have a jack and a spare. I'll call you later."

She ended the call with Beckett and went back out onto the highway. A semi-truck screamed by, and the draft from the truck shook her car. Geez. The cold wind blew through her parka, and a shiver rocked her body. She opened the trunk to pull out her tools and heaved the spare out onto the snow. She rolled the tire to the side of the road and checked the directions in the manual.

The first thing she had to do was loosen the lug nuts with the crowbar. She fit the crowbar to the lug nut, but when she pulled, the lug nut didn't move. She tried one more time and yanked—hard. She fell on her butt in the slushy snow and growled. With the wind whipping snow in her face, she got up and rubbed her hands together, ready to try again.

She fastened the crowbar to the lug nut and put all her weight into it. She could hear her dad saying "lefty loosey, righty tighty," but it didn't matter which way she tried to force it, nothing budged. She hopped back into the car to warm her hands before giving it another try. She glanced at her phone on the dashboard. Should she call for help? After a long moment of indecision, she shook her head. No. She could do this. She pushed back outside, grabbed the crowbar, and secured it around the lug nut. Another truck blew by, and then a smaller truck rumbled past her and slowed. The truck drove to the shoulder and backed up with an obnoxious beeping noise. Penny stood still, holding the tool. A guy jumped out of the truck and headed toward her with a clipboard in his hand.

"Penny O'Brien?"

"Yeah."

"Blown tire?"

"Yep. I can't get the lug nuts off. I have a spare, though. How'd you know I was here?"

The man flipped a page and said, "Beckett Young ordered the truck. I'm to change the tire or tow you to the nearest mechanic. Looks like a straightforward tire change. Give me ten minutes."

Penny paced back and forth in front of her car as the tow truck guy got to work. She punched Beckett's name on her phone. He picked up on the first ring.

"What're you doing?" said Penny. "I told you I had every-thing under control."

"You're mad?"

"I can take care of myself."

"It's after nine o'clock at night. You're stranded on the side of a highway in Minnesota—in *February*. I couldn't sit here in my warm condo and hope for the best."

"I'm not a princess you need to rescue from the tower."

"You were in trouble. I care about you. I was worried."

Penny stood silent and replayed his words in her head. *He cared about her?* "All set ma'am," said the tow truck driver, interrupting her thoughts.

"I gotta go." She hung up with Beckett and said, "How much do I owe you?" to the tow truck driver.

"It's covered." The man returned to his truck, and Penny slid into her car. She blasted the heat and blew on her hands to thaw her fingers.

Two hours later, she climbed the metal stairs and opened the door to a freezing apartment. She kicked the radiator, and it sputtered to life. Shivering in her bed, Beckett's words repeated in her head again. He cared about her? Worried? Is that why he wanted to give her brand new ice skates and save her on the side of the highway? If he was stranded or needed something, would she hesitate to help him? No. Then why was it so hard for her to accept his help?

She pulled her phone off the crate beside her bed and texted him, *Sorry.*

Her phone rang immediately.

"Are you alright? Home?" asked Beckett.

His smooth voice brought tears to her eyes. "I'm home. Sorry. I'm not used to leaning on anyone, and I like to do things for myself."

"I get it. Glad you're safe."

"Thanks. See you next Friday."

"Bye, Penny."

Chapter Twelve

Deicing delayed the family plane on the tarmac in Cincinnati. Beckett groaned and dug around in his duffle for his book. His hand hit the gift he bought Penny for Valentine's Day. He still didn't know if it was the right gift.

He had spent two weeks thinking of a Valentine's gift for Penny. He wanted to buy her jewelry but thought it was too soon. His mind wandered to lingerie. Definitely too soon. Then he thought of something practical, like a warm winter coat or an emergency kit for her car, but as much as she needed those things, he didn't think she'd appreciate them. So, he settled on tickets to *Hamilton* in Minneapolis. He booked dinner at a five-star restaurant and a penthouse suite in a hotel. If their relationship didn't last until the show, she could take a friend, and he'd cancel the other arrangements. He usually didn't stay in relationships long enough to hit a holiday or birthday, so this was all new territory for him.

The pilot announced take off. Beckett put the card and tickets back in his duffle, and found his book. His stomach heaved from bumping around in the clouds, but he thanked his crew when they landed. Beckett rented a car and drove to Misty Lake. The curves and ice patches on the road delayed his arrival, and Penny texted him she was in the park about to perform. He parked the car in her driveway before pulling on his hat and gloves and walking to the festival.

Pink and red hearts hung from the lamp posts, twinkling lights greeting him as he strolled down the sidewalk. A big banner touted the *Love Snow Festival*, and steam from kettle corn and grilled sausages filled the air. Elementary school children worked to build snowmen for some sort of contest, and Penny's voice drifted over the crowd in the park.

Beckett bumped into Drew. The men shook hands and pulled each other into a bro hug. "Hey man. Welcome back to Misty Lake," said Drew.

Beckett turned and nodded to Kelly. "Nice to see you again, Kelly."

"Good to see you, Beckett."

Mark and Emma joined the group in the park while Penny entertained the crowd. She sang under the pergola—which had been wrapped in twinkling lights—and locked eyes with him as she crooned into the mic. The lights bounced off her face—she shined like a star in the darkening sky. Although people and noise surrounded him, the world faded away as her voice penetrated his soul.

After her set, Penny thanked the crowd and placed the mic on its stand. She bounded toward him. Every minute of his long day of travel was worth it to hold Penny in his arms.

"Sorry I was late," said Beckett. "The plane sat on the tarmac forever in Cincinnati."

Penny sighed against him. "Glad you made it."

Beckett kissed Penny's cheek. "Let's grab dinner."

Penny steered him toward the best pizza he'd ever eaten in

his life. Then, they followed it up with dessert. "Wow. This is delicious," he said.

"It's a funnel cake. Fried dough."

"My first."

"You're kidding? What did you eat at the state fair?"

"I've never been to a state fair."

"County fair?"

Beckett shook his head.

"4-H event?"

"What's that?"

Penny looped her arm through his and laughed.

They strolled through the raffle and bought hot chocolate. The freezing temperatures didn't bother him with Penny snuggling against him all night. Later, he pulled Penny into the photo booth, and they posed for silly pictures. They smashed their cheeks together and smiled. One photo was of Penny laughing with her head thrown back. Another captured him kissing her on the nose. After the machine spit out their strip of photos, he stuffed them into his jacket pocket. She leaned into him and said, "Let's go."

* * *

Penny had enough of the festival and wanted to be alone with Beckett. He didn't take his eyes off her for the whole set, and her breasts swelled inside her parka. They hurried back to her apartment, and her stomach flip-flopped as they climbed the steps. Her apartment was tiny and sparse. She didn't know where he lived, but a good guess would be: not above a garage. He probably had cars bigger than her home. Oh, well, too late now. She unlocked the door and gave it a shove with her shoulder before she turned to put her hand on his chest, stopping him from entering.

"My apartment is small. I mean, like, super small. It's clean but tiny."

Beckett put his hand over hers and said, "I don't care how big your apartment is. I'm here to be with you."

Her chest fluttered. She clicked on the overhead light, and they stepped inside. They took off their coats and hats and tossed them on the table. She grabbed his arm and pulled him toward her. Every time their lips joined, a new story unfolded. She craved him like a drug. They angled their heads and found a new position. The kiss intensified to a fevered rate until he took a breath and kissed along her jaw. When he drew her silky earlobe into his mouth, Penny gasped from the new sensation.

Penny wrapped her leg around his thigh and pulled him closer. "I know you have a room at Northern Woods, but can you stay for a while?"

"I'll stay as long as you'll have me."

She tugged him to her bed—there was no other place to be in the small space. They fell onto the pillows and faced one another. Beckett placed his lips against hers. She trailed her hand down his shirt and released the buttons one at a time. When she reached the last button, she pushed the fabric away from his body but not off his arms. Her hands roamed over his smooth skin, discovering the shape of his chest. When her fingers grazed a nipple, goosebumps spread across his muscles.

Beckett cupped her breast through her bulky sweater, but she was desperate to feel his hands on her skin. She broke their kiss and sat up on the bed. "Lay on your back," she whispered to him. He tossed his unbuttoned shirt to the floor while she sat up on her knees and straddled his thighs. She traced the outline of his bare shoulders and shivered on top of him. The moon spilled through the thin curtain on her window and cast a white glow across her body. Without breaking eye contact, she lifted off her sweater and dropped it on the floor. Her heart hammered against her chest. Never in her life had she been so forward with a guy.

Her swollen breasts filled her favorite black bra. Desperate for touch, she picked up one of his hands and placed it against her hot flesh. Beckett held their weight and rubbed his thumbs over her stiff nipples. Their hips rocked against each other in response. When he slipped a finger under the straps of her bra, they fell down her arms, exposing more of her milky, white skin.

Penny dated enough men to know her breast size aroused them, but she usually kept the groping to a minimum. This time, however, she needed more from Beckett. She unhooked the bra and let it slide to the floor. She tossed her hair behind her shoulders, and silence filled the room. Beckett's eyes dilated as he teased her nipples into rocks.

"Glorious." he said in a reverent whisper.

Desperate for skin-to-skin contact, she sank on top of him, and they sighed together when her breasts yielded against his bare chest. Beckett rolled them to their sides. He bent down and pulled a nipple between his lips. He circled the nub with his tongue, and shocks pulsed her core. Desperate for more, she offered up her other breast, and he repeated his ministrations. Penny moaned and clasped a hand over her mouth.

"What's wrong?" asked Beckett.

Penny's chest flushed a dark pink. "Sorry." She'd never moaned while a guy kissed her breast, and she wasn't sure why it happened.

Beckett let go of her nipple, and his lips worked their way down her cleavage. "Never be sorry," he said in between kisses, "moan, sigh, and groan all you want. It helps me learn what you like."

All of a sudden, her heart raced—she stopped moving. Beckett was going to want sex. It was too soon. Should she tell him about her virginity and send him back to Northern Woods? Every cell in her body wanted him to stay with her, though. She wanted to explore more of him. What should she do?

"Penny?"

"Yeah?"

"Where did you go?"

"Oh, um . . ."

"We can stop."

"No. It's just . . ."

"You lead. I'll follow."

Those four words calmed her heart rate and gave her time to weigh her options. With the three basic choices of all, none, or somewhere in between, Penny opted for somewhere in between. With her decision made, she reached a hand between them and shoved his jeans down his legs. She sat up and whipped off her leggings. Lying beside one another in minimal clothing, he peppered her with kisses along her neck and collarbone while exploring the soft skin of her inner thighs with his fingers. He grazed the last bit of fabric covering her skin, and she squirmed until he moved it aside and touched her throbbing flesh. Penny groaned into his mouth and wrapped a hand around his erection. The tiny window beside the bed fogged, and the cold night was forgotten.

Chapter Thirteen

Beckett spooned her as the gray of dawn blinked awake outside of her window. His faint snores filled her small room. Warmth flooded her limbs when she remembered the previous night. She'd never been so bold in all her life, but the desire to be close to Beckett engulfed her. Her longtime belief to wait for sex was fading fast—she needed to clear her head. Six thirty. Beth would be working in the café, but it wouldn't be open yet. Penny slid out of bed, and Beckett turned over and mumbled something. She bent down and kissed him on the cheek. "Going to grab coffee. I'll be back."

"Hmm."

She donned her leggings and a sweatshirt and grabbed her parka and hat off the table. Flurries fell from the sky, coating the park with fresh white fluff. Low light glowed from behind the café's counter. Penny cupped her hands over her eyes and peered through the glass. Spotting movement inside, she knocked on the door. Beth waved to her before holding up a finger for her to wait. A minute later, Beth unlocked the dead bolt and let her inside the warm café.

"You're up early. Coffee?" asked Beth.

Penny held up two fingers. "To go."

Beth's eyes widened, and her mouth formed a perfect O. "Beckett?"

Penny nodded. "He spent the night."

"Wow. Did you...um...aren't you a . . ."

Penny held up her hand. "No. We didn't go all the way, but we messed around a bunch."

She followed Beth behind the counter and perched on a stool beside the desk. Beth put two large coffees with three creams and one sugar on the counter. Penny wrapped her hands around one of the cups and closed her eyes to inhale the steaming liquid.

"You're a genius."

"Thanks." Beth sat on the other stool. "Was it amazing?"

Penny's face broke out in a wide smile. "I've never experienced anything like this before. If I could've climbed inside of him, we wouldn't have been close enough. The connection was magnetic."

Beth fanned herself with a towel. Penny continued. "He's so kind and thoughtful, and we talk about everything. We agree on a lot of stuff, but...he's older, and he's got the adulting thing figured out. The biggest difference between us is money—I don't have much, and he has a ton...or, at least, I think he does. I mean, who owns four winter coats?"

"Don't dwell on the differences. Focus on how you feel about each other."

"Should I tell him I'm a virgin? The last guy I told freaked out and never called me again."

"Beckett seems more mature than that, but it's up to you. He might appreciate the heads up, though."

Kelly knocked on the café door, and Beth popped off the

stool to greet her. "Give me a sec?" Beth called over her shoulder to Penny.

"Take your time," said Penny.

Cold air followed Kelly inside as she made three trips from her car to the café to unload the trays of pastries. Beth began filling her display cases with the yeasty treats.

Penny sipped the hot coffee while her friends worked. Her mind trailed to Beckett and his talented lips and fingers. A new flutter filled her chest as she recalled her body turning to putty in his hands. She needed to tell him about her virginity. Beth was right—he was mature enough to handle the news.

"Did you have fun last night?" Kelly asked Penny.

Penny's head snapped up, and she smiled at Kelly. "Oh...yeah."

Beth filled the last display case as Kelly raised a playful eyebrow at Penny. "I thought you and Beckett were going to combust. The heat coming off you two—whew."

Penny blushed. "Beth, can I have two of those bear claws to go?" She plunked her money on the counter.

"I'm guessing I won't see Beckett at breakfast in the lodge this morning?" asked Kelly.

Penny's pink cheeks turned red—she shook her head. "Beth can fill you in on the details." She grabbed the coffees and pastries. "Thanks." She went back outside to the cold, quiet town.

She set the coffees and pastries on the table before hanging her parka on the hook. Beckett blinked open his eyes. "Morning," he said. "C'mere."

Penny sat on the bed beside him and bent down for a kiss. Her hair spilled over their faces, creating a private tent. Her chilly lips met his warm ones, and they melted together in a tender kiss.

Beckett sighed as she placed a hand on his cheek. "I have coffee," said Penny.

"Excellent." Beckett jumped out of bed and slipped on his shirt and jeans. Penny blushed when she remembered how her aggressiveness had led to his clothes spending the night on her floor.

She folded two paper towels into napkins and set a bear claw on each one. Beckett swiped a hand through his hair and joined Penny at the table. He took a huge bite of a bear claw and gulped his coffee. "I can't believe this small town has such amazing food."

"I know. People come to experience the Boundary Waters and get the food as a bonus," said Penny.

"I've been learning more about the Boundary Waters while setting up Helen's nonprofit. Did you know there are companies who want to mine the minerals there? If they're allowed, it'll pollute the water and disrupt the natural habitats. It's toxic. Fighting those huge companies takes a ton of money. I don't know a lot about it, but I'm learning."

"Yep. There are a bunch of environmental nonprofits who work to keep the area natural and clean. How's the fundraiser idea coming along?"

"Great. The board voted on a venue and caterer. There's going to be a silent auction, and two members of the board are in charge of the guest list and invitations."

"Progress."

"I suppose. I had an idea to label miniature canoe paddles as name plates. What do you think of that?"

"Super cute. I was at a wedding last summer where the centerpieces were fairy lights inside of candle votives instead of actual candles. Magical."

"Great idea. Let me jot that down." He pulled out his phone and made a note.

Penny cleaned up their breakfast.

"What should we do today?" asked Beckett.

"Let's watch the hockey tournament at Northern Woods. We can hike in the forest, too. It's warmer today."

"You mean it's almost zero?"

Penny snorted. "Something like that."

Penny drove them to Northern Woods. She slowed on the icy gravel drive and growled at the full parking lot.

"Let's turn around," said Beckett. "I think there's overflow parking back there." He pointed up the gravel drive.

"I've got this," said Penny. She maneuvered her car toward the edge of the parking lot.

"What're you doing? There are piles of snow everywhere."

"Relax." She pulled forward beside a car and started parallel parking. The open spot was full of snow, but she gunned the engine and angled it in. She pulled forward again and bumped the car in front of her.

"Aah! You hit the car!"

She backed up a foot. "Just a tap. It's fine." She turned off the engine and smiled at Beckett.

* * *

Beckett cringed at the body slamming on the ice, and the intense hockey game had Penny hollering swear words at the opposing team. While watching the game from the bench by the shore, he developed a new respect for the sport. Doing anything on that thin blade took serious skill.

After a short hike in the woods and lunch in the lodge, they returned to her car, wedged in the snowbank. A note flapped on her windshield. Penny groaned and grabbed the paper. Back in the car, she handed him the note from the Northern Woods staff asking her to use the overflow parking next time. "Throw it in the glove box."

Beckett opened the glove box, and a pile of traffic tickets fell into his hands. "Penny, have you paid these tickets?"

She inched the car forward and backward, trying to get out of the space while her bald tires spun on the snow. "What? Oh. Those? No. They're just parking tickets. The Misty Lake sheriff is a real stickler about clearing the streets for plows and stuff."

He counted the tickets and added up the fines. "You have, like, a hundred and thirty dollars in fines."

"It's fine. I'll get around to it."

He organized the tickets by date and stacked them into a neat pile before returning them to the glove box. Who was this woman? Penny's enormous personality had him reeling. They'd spent the night together, and he barely touched her before she exploded. He couldn't get enough of her endless curves and soft skin, and their lips were in love with each other. Her supple body melded perfectly against his, like she was created to be his match.

He wasn't used to being with such an independent woman. She did crazy stuff with her car and refused his help, even when stranded on the side of a freeway. Penny's self-reliance frightened and excited him at the same time. He couldn't wait to learn more about her.

* * *

Penny styled her hair and applied her makeup before changing into her dark green dress for another Love Snow Festival performance in the park. She turned her back to Beckett and asked, "Can you zip me up?"

"Of course." He set his phone down on the dining table and came up behind her. His fingers moved her hair to one shoulder, and he zipped the dress. Lips nuzzled her bare neck, and she leaned into him and sighed. His hand followed the slope of her hip all the way up to her breast. She turned around and wrapped her arms around his neck, capturing his lips in a kiss.

"Why can't I get enough of you?" she murmured.

In between kisses, he said, "Same."

Penny leaned into the kiss and ran her hands down his back.

He pulled her closer to him, and their legs pressed together. After another deep kiss, he pulled back and pressed his forehead to hers. "I have to tell you something."

A lump formed in her throat, and she struggled to swallow. They'd just started dating, what could be wrong? Was he sick? Going to break up with her? But he didn't pull away—he held her tight in his arms.

"I don't think I've ever experienced such intense emotions with a woman before. I've never had a serious relationship and usually don't date much beyond a few dinners and a weekend away with a woman. But with you, the feelings are...different."

Penny scanned his concerned face. She didn't know how to respond to him, so she said, "As long as we're being honest, I have something to share, too."

He held her close. "Go ahead."

It took a long moment before the words tumbled out of her mouth. "I'm a virgin."

* * *

A virgin? Beckett flashed back to last night. Did he do anything to make her feel uncomfortable? As an adult, he'd never dated a virgin. His first time was with a woman three years older and a million times more mature. Penny was five years younger than him at twenty-two, but all the women he dated before her had lost their virginity in high school or college. Did she never have a serious relationship? Or was a belief holding her back? Rage bubbled up through his core—did someone hurt her?

He wandered around the festival raffle until Penny started her set. The sound of her voice lilting over the din did weird things to his gut, and he returned to the park to join the rest of the crowd. She commanded the stage, and the crowd sang the popular cover songs along with her. When she finished her set, a roar of applause followed, and she took her bows.

After the next performance group started, Penny found Beckett in the crowd, and he brought her into his arms. They danced on the edge of the makeshift dance floor, away from other couples.

"That was a pretty big confession I dropped on you," said Penny. "I have to know what you're thinking."

He gazed into her eyes. "I'm thinking you're amazing, and I feel lucky to have met you. I'm thinking you'll tell me more if you want to. I'm thinking any time I have with you is precious and special. I'm thinking...I hope no one hurt you."

She pressed closer to him as they danced. "No one hurt me. I've just always wanted to wait until I fell in love."

He inhaled a breath. *Love? She planned to wait until she was in love?* Oh, man. As someone who'd never uttered those words to another woman, he didn't have a response.

"I just never found the right guy."

Beckett pulled her closer to him when the song changed. His hands wandered across her back, and he hugged her tight. A million questions went through his mind, but Penny whispered, "Every minute I spend with you is my favorite," into his ear. He decided, then, to take their relationship day by day and enjoy Penny in the moment.

When he cupped Penny's backside, a man thumped Beckett on the shoulder and said, "This is a family festival, buddy." They stifled a laugh and hurried back to Penny's apartment.

* * *

After another night of kissing, touching, and talking, Penny's feelings for Beckett multiplied, and she didn't want him to leave. The realization of a long-distance relationship hit her hard as they stirred awake in her bed. Did the relationship have any chance? They lived so far apart.

She had always thought her first serious relationship would be with someone who lived in the same city or town. They'd go to the movies on the weekend or meet for coffee in the middle of the week. They'd hang out at each other's apartments and listen to music or go camping or to a concert together, but it wasn't like that with Beckett. Their relationship depended on phone calls, texts, and video chats. He'd traveled to Misty Lake three times in the last month. Surely, he couldn't keep buying flights.

"Happy Valentine's Day," said Beckett.

She snuggled against him. "Happy Valentine's Day. I have something for you."

"Me, too."

She kissed him and tossed her leg over his thigh. "Later."

Penny's skin glistened with sweat after Beckett's hands danced across her. "You need to go soon."

Beckett lay flat on his back and sighed. "Yeah."

She wrapped a sheet around her body and dug his gift out of a drawer in the kitchenette. He fished his gift out of his duffle. They exchanged, and he said, "Ladies first."

She smiled and opened the card. Two tickets to *Hamilton* spilled into her hands. "Ooh! I've wanted to see this for two years." Tears pooled in her eyes. She kissed him. "Thank you."

"I've made dinner and hotel reservations, but if you want to take a different friend or get separate rooms or . . ."

She put a finger on his lips. "I want to go with you and stay in one room. Thank you."

He swallowed and nodded. He pulled open the strings of the velvet pouch she'd handed him. A silver keychain in the shape of a loon dangled from his fingers. "I love it. Now a piece of the north woods will always be with me."

Two hours later, Penny clung to Beckett in her driveway. "I've never had such a hard time saying goodbye."

"We'll meet in two weeks for *Hamilton*," said Beckett. "In the meantime, we'll call, text, and facetime." He kissed her one last time and drove away.

His taillights disappeared around the corner, and Penny hugged herself in the driveway. Why did she feel like Beckett just drove off with a huge part of her soul?

Chapter Fourteen

On the last day of February in Minneapolis, the beat reverberated through Penny's theater box seat. Penny leaned forward toward the balcony to get as close as she could to the stage where *Hamilton* played out before their eyes. Beckett reached for her elbow, urging her back into her seat—he probably thought she was going to topple over the edge. She smiled at him and sat back an inch. The actors, dancing, and music all reignited her lifelong passion for theater. She ached to be back on the stage.

After the show, Penny clutched Beckett's hand and skipped up the sidewalk on the dark, cold night.

"Wasn't that the best? I want to be back on the stage. I need to be back on stage. When I was in high school and college, I was always either in the middle of a show or auditioning for a show. There was never a break. Singing in restaurants and at weddings is great, but I want more. The rush of the story and drama of the cast." She sighed and leaned into Beckett.

"How do you remember all the words? And where to go on the stage? I would be a nervous wreck."

Penny smiled. "Rehearsals. Tons of rehearsals. But those are fun, too. The cast becomes your family." They rounded the corner to their hotel. She stopped on the street and pulled Beckett against her chest. "Thank you for the best night I've had in a long time." She went onto her tiptoes and kissed him until they lost themselves in each other. A police siren wailed past them, and they startled apart, but Penny didn't take her eyes off him. "Let's go upstairs."

"I thought you wanted to try the new wine bar?" said Beckett.

"Changed my mind." She kissed him again and ran her tongue along his lower lip.

When the hotel elevator doors swished closed, Penny's desire for Beckett piqued. After two weeks without him, she yearned for him. She pushed him up against the side wall and pressed her lips against his while her fingers worked his overcoat buttons. The elevator *binged*—they separated before the doors swished open. Beckett panted and nodded hello to an older couple. Penny stood still beside him, but her hand worked its way around his waist. She snaked her fingers inside the top of his suit pants and under his shirt until she reached warm skin. A young woman joined the group in the elevator, and they were pushed further back toward the wall.

Penny moved two fingers up and down along an inch of his hip bone, and Beckett stifled a moan as the older couple exited the elevator. The doors closed. While the young woman scrolled on her phone, Penny scraped a fingernail along his skin —he covered his yelp with a cough, and Penny chuckled beside him. She loved giving in to her feelings and discovering new ways to excite both of them. The woman left the elevator, and they were alone again.

Beckett tugged her against his body. "You've touched two square inches of my skin, tops. How is it that I've never been so turned on in all my life?"

She grinned and kissed him. When the elevator *binged* on the top floor, Penny blew out a breath. "Finally."

Once inside the hotel room, they tossed their coats on a nearby chair. Penny kicked off her heels and began to unzip her dress when Beckett stopped her. In between nips on her cheeks and chin, Beckett reached behind her and unzipped her dress inch by inch until her back was bare. He returned to her lips for a long, soul-drenching kiss before unclipping her hair from its style. Penny urged him out of his suit coat and angled her neck toward him as he worked his magic on the spot below her ear. A low groan bubbled up and out of her mouth.

Penny loosened his tie, and it slithered to the floor. She shimmied her hips, and her dress puddled to their feet. When she stepped out of it and stood before him in her black, silk bodysuit, Beckett inhaled. It was her one and only piece of true lingerie—sexy, yet comfortable—and with her thigh-high stockings, it lengthened her already long legs.

"Wow," Beckett whispered.

"Thanks," said Penny as she unbuttoned his dress shirt and kissed his collarbone.

He ran his hands up and down the silky material while she rid him of his suit pants. Then he led her to the bed where she settled onto the hard planes of his chest and thighs. He rolled them over, and their kisses deepened with each breath. Her hips rocked against his with a mind of their own. He stripped off her bodysuit, and they lay skin to skin under the sheets.

She needed more of him and wanted his lips everywhere on her body. Every bone in her body demanded more from Beckett. She pushed his shoulders again, but he stopped. "Are you sure?"

Swirling with warmth, she nodded. He kissed his way down her breasts and past her belly before settling between her legs. The sensitive skin of her inner thighs heated until she thought they would burst into flames. She squirmed under him as his lips kissed their way to her center. The new sensations were like nothing she'd ever experienced—they sent rocket fuel coursing through her body. She shouted her release too soon.

He climbed up her body and held her tight. "Are you alright?"

She laughed, breathless. "I've crossed over into heaven. Join me." She traveled down his body and gave in to her instincts.

Hours later, they lay in bed, satiated and entwined together. She licked her swollen lips as Beckett brushed the hair off her face. She stared at him. She couldn't believe this wonderful man had come into her life. He was so different from any other guy she'd ever dated—patient, kind, and giving. Their attraction was undeniable. Heat surged in her chest, and she couldn't hold it back any longer. "I think I'm falling in love with you, Beckett."

Chapter Fifteen

A LONE ON A DARK WEDNESDAY MORNING, four days after taking Penny to *Hamilton*, Beckett rolled over in bed. A nightmare had woken him, and he couldn't get back to sleep. He ached for Penny.

They'd dated for two months, the longest he'd ever been with a woman. Penny was also his first long-distance relationship. She had told him she was falling in love with him the night of *Hamilton*. He'd kissed her but hadn't responded. He was so stupid. He loved Penny. There was no doubt in his mind.

Penny had kicked her dance and voice training into high gear to audition for a show in Cleveland, but they managed to talk on the phone at least once a day and to video chat late at night. He sat up in bed. He needed to see her. All of a sudden, nothing mattered more than telling her he loved her—but he wanted to tell her in person.

What was stopping him? He had the ability to fly anywhere at a moment's notice. He grabbed his phone off the nightstand and opened his calendar—a regular work day and no basketball games. With a few clicks through his phone, before the sun rose, he scheduled a half-day off from work and arranged for his plane and driver. After securing his travel, he packed a bag and went into the office. If the timing worked out, he'd be in Misty Lake just as Penny got off work. During his morning break, he called Northern Woods to book a suite with a jacuzzi tub. She'd love a surprise mid-week soak.

He boarded his plane at one o'clock in the afternoon. The pilot warned him of possible turbulence in the upper Midwest. Beckett decided to put in his earbuds, and after take-off, his flight attendant brought him a snack. He dozed off once they reached cruising altitude.

Beckett woke an hour later to the plane knocking him around. He grabbed the seat in front of him.

"Mr. Young, we've hit some rough air," said the pilot. "Please make sure your safety belt is secured, and stow anything loose under your seat. Flight attendants, please buckle into your jump seats until we reach a better altitude."

The plane swooped to one side and knocked about. Beckett bounced around in his seat and started to sweat. Penny—he needed to tell her he loved her. He closed his eyes and envisioned her singing and dancing with him. Another bump caused his body to lift from the seat. He held his head in his hands and breathed deep. He pictured Penny with her arms and legs wrapped around him as he peppered her with kisses.

The pilot leveled the plane for a few minutes, allowing Beckett to catch his breath. He stole a glance out the window at the swirling, white sky. Why did he wait? Why didn't he tell Penny he loved her when he had the chance? The jet dipped and bumped again—Beckett gripped his arm rests, and the flight attendant gave a little *yip* from her seat. After what felt like an eternity, they began their descent to the Duluth airport. The plane jostled all the way to the slick runway. Once stopped, he gathered his bag and removed some bills from his wallet.

He shook the pilot's hand on the way out the door and slid three hundred dollars into the man's hand. "Tonight's on me. I appreciate you and your crew." The pilot nodded his thanks.

Beckett entered the car waiting on the tarmac. As the driver began the journey away from the airport, Beckett rested his head against the leather seat.

The ride to Misty Lake took longer than usual. He asked the driver to go straight to Penny's apartment. Her car wasn't in the drive, but he knocked on her door anyway. The dark apartment confirmed she wasn't there, so he asked the driver to take them to Drew's office. Penny's car wasn't in front of the law office either, but Drew's light glowed from the bay window. He knocked on the door.

"Beckett?" asked Drew when he opened the door. "Did we have a meeting?"

"No. I'm looking for Penny. She's not at home. I thought she might be here."

"She didn't mention anything about a visit."

Beckett shifted from foot to foot. "It's a surprise."

"Aah. Got it. She's at the church rehearsing with her old dance teacher. She took off early for the lesson." He glanced at his watch. "She's probably almost done."

Beckett shook Drew's hand. "Thanks."

He got back into the car and directed the driver to the church. The front door was locked, so he walked around the side. He followed the sound of music echoing from down the hall. His heart pounded in his chest. After the harrowing flight, all he wanted to do was tell her he loved her and wrap her into his arms. But when he approached the room, he found Penny in the arms of another man.

Chapter Sixteen

Sweat glistened on Penny's body as she danced the routine over and over again. Her dance teacher called out the steps, and she did her best to follow his instructions. When their two-hour session came to an end, tears pricked her eyes. She was out of shape, and her muscles throbbed from the hard workout.

Her teacher killed the music, though didn't say anything. When he opened his arms, she didn't hesitate to accept the warm embrace. She cried on his shoulder while he rubbed her back and said, "You'll get there. Keep practicing. You can do it."

"Penny?"

Penny yanked her body from her dance teacher and turned toward the door. Beckett stood on the threshold with a pained look on his face. "Beckett? What're you doing here?"

He cleared his throat. "I came to see you. You're busy. I'll go." He spun on his heel and disappeared. Penny gently squeezed her teacher's arm. "Can you give me a minute?"

She chased Beckett down the hallway, catching him before he pushed out the door. "If I'd known you were coming, I wouldn't have scheduled a class."

"I wanted to surprise you, but I guess the surprise is on me."

Penny scrunched up her nose. "Not sure what you mean by that, but give me ten minutes to finish up, and I'll meet you somewhere."

"I've got a suite at Northern Woods."

"You came all this way and don't want to stay with me?"

Beckett sighed. "Come to Northern Woods when you're done. I'll text you the room number." He pushed out the church door into the chilly night and got into the back seat of his town car. The sleek car pulled away from the curb and disappeared from sight.

* * *

Beckett felt as though a jack hammer pounded his head after his long day. He and Penny never had a conversation about exclusivity; he just assumed. Was Penny seeing the dance teacher? Their bodies could've been one with how tight she clung to his Lycra-covered limbs. Waves of jealousy rolled through him like an angry ocean—he chastised himself for getting so serious so fast with Penny. Add in the long distance, and it was not a sustainable situation.

Beckett checked into the lodge and rode the elevator to the third floor. He collapsed on the bed and waited. A half hour later, a soft knock sounded on the door. He opened it, and Penny stood before him with tear-stained cheeks and red-rimmed eyes. He expected her to be angry and defensive. What he didn't expect was the sheer sadness that covered her face. She flopped onto the chair in the corner and cradled her knees in her arms.

"What's wrong? Are you mad because I surprised you? Or that I caught you with another man?"

Penny's head snapped up. "Mad? I'm not mad. Surprised you're here, yes, but not mad. I'm frustrated with my dancing. And I was with my teacher, not some other man."

Beckett paced the room. "He was wrapped around you like a snake catching its prey."

Penny rested her head back down on her knees. Was she crying? When she raised her head, tears streamed down her face, but her body shook with laughter.

"Why're you laughing?"

Penny rose from the chair and pulled him to the edge of the bed. She sniffled and picked up his hand. "Let's start from the beginning. Why are you here?"

Beckett yanked his hand back. "I missed you like crazy this morning. I was lying in bed and thought it would be fun to surprise you with dinner and a soak in a jacuzzi." He pressed his lips together. "I couldn't find you at home, and Drew said you'd be at the church with your dance teacher. I didn't expect you to be in the arms of another man."

Penny nodded. "Okay. My turn. I asked my old dance teacher to help me with my routine before the Cleveland audition. He drove from Minneapolis to teach me today. I was frustrated by the end of our session because I'm out of practice, and my muscles burned. We're old friends, and he comforted me."

Beckett growled. "He had his hands all over you."

"He's been a friend forever," Penny smirked. "Besides, I could never replace his husband."

Beckett was about to say something and then stopped. "Oh."

"Now that we have that straight, I'm super excited you're here for the night and splurged on a suite with a tub. My muscles need some love."

Beckett picked up her hand. "Sorry."

"It's okay. The long-distance sucks sometimes."

Beckett ordered dinner. After a long talk over clam chowder and homemade biscuits, they were back to normal.

Beckett helped her out of her dance clothes and into the tub. He slid in behind her and turned on the jets. She sank against his chest, and he kissed the top of her head.

"I need to tell you something," said Beckett.

"Okay."

"This morning, when I cooked up my crazy idea to surprise you, it was because I had to tell you how much I love you. I didn't want to tell you over the phone, and I couldn't wait." Penny gasped and turned to face him in the tub. "Later, the plane ran into severe turbulence. It was bad. We lost altitude, and we were jostled around in our seats. I've never in my life had such a rough flight."

Penny placed a hand on his chest. "Oh, no."

"The whole time we bumped around, all I could think about was you and how I needed for you to know how much I love you. I'm in love with you, Penny O'Brien."

Chapter Seventeen

THE EARLY SPRING snow crunched under her boots on the way to work. The crisp air filled her lungs, and her pastry oozed sweetness from its bag. After Beckett had told her he loved her, she wanted to burst open like the new buds on the trees.

She hummed the chorus of a song from the musical *Evita* as she rounded the park in the center of town. Penny's desire to be on stage consumed her. She immersed herself in the history of Eva Perón, learning everything about the woman who became the wife of an Argentinian president. She spent every free moment singing and dancing to prepare for her audition to play Evita.

A week later, Penny paced the airport terminal in Duluth. Weather delayed her flight to Cleveland for the audition, and panic bubbled in her chest. She didn't want to miss the flight.

After the gate agent announced another delay, Penny called Beckett.

"Are you in Cleveland?" he asked.

"Flight keeps getting delayed. I'm losing my mind. I spent too much on this flight and can't miss the audition."

"I can arrange a flight for you."

"What? No, you can't. This is the only flight to Cleveland out of Duluth tonight."

"Let me help you."

"You're helping me by talking with me."

"How about I meet you in Cleveland tomorrow?"

"No. I don't need any distractions."

"I'm not a distraction."

Penny laughed. "Yes, you are. They're calling my plane to board. Finally."

"Good luck. Call me tomorrow."

The following day, Beckett spent his lunch hour at an upscale jewelry store. The saleswoman steered him toward sapphire necklaces, but he chose emerald to match Penny's eyes. He'd never spent so much time looking for the perfect gift for a woman. The heavy jewel felt cool against his palm. He couldn't wait to give it to her.

The pre-audition vocal warm-up and dance routine was standard, but union actors with glossy resumes filled the stage. A lead role was impossible.

Penny auditioned for a role in the company, but the competition was so fierce that she was cut and sent home. She stumbled out of the theater and plugged in her information for a rideshare to the airport. On her way to the airport, in the back seat of a dirty car, she called Beckett.

"Penny?"

As soon as she heard his voice, a sob erupted—she cried into the phone. His smooth voice calmed her, and she sniffled, "I was cut before lunch. The director told me to go home and work in community theater to build my resume. I don't have an agent, and I'm not in the union, either."

"Union?"

"Yeah. The stage actor's union. I can't afford it yet, but I guess you have to be a member to have a shot at the bigger roles in regional productions."

"I'm sorry."

"It's okay. I should've known better. I'm at the airport. I'll call when I land."

"Love you."

"I love you."

The uneventful flight landed on time in Duluth, but the aircraft took forever to deplane. Irritation grated her nerves. She needed to be home where she could curl up in bed and lose herself to sleep. When she made it to baggage claim, she stopped and blinked. Beckett stood beside the carousel with his hands in his pockets. What was he doing in Duluth?

When he saw her, he opened his arms and tilted his head. Tears filled her eyes, and she ran into his embrace.

"I'm so sorry, Penny. Let's go home."

Penny slumped against the passenger window of her car and shivered because the heat only worked part time. Beckett let her talk and process her failure without judging her. When they arrived, he helped carry her luggage up the staircase, and she disappeared into the bathroom. After a hot shower, she changed into his T-shirt and climbed into bed beside him. There weren't a lot of words, but he held her tight.

. . .

The following morning, her cold nose and frozen toes were clear signs the heat had failed again in her apartment. Penny shivered against Beckett even though his arm wrapped around her body. She groaned and wiggled out from his embrace. A shiver coursed through her body as her bare feet hit the hardwood. A quick check of the cold and silent radiator confirmed her suspicion.

"Penny? It's freezing," Beckett grumbled, half-awake.

"Yeah, sorry. Give me a minute." She grabbed the wrench she kept on her crate and tightened the connection between the valve and the pipe, but it only clanged to life after she'd given it a swift kick. She hopped back into bed to snuggle against Beckett. She lay her head on his chest, and he ran his hand up and down her back.

"Where did you learn how to do that?"

She laughed. "Who *doesn't* know how to do that?" She lifted her head off his chest. "Thanks for meeting me last night. I didn't realize how much I needed you until you were there."

"I didn't want to be anywhere else. I'll work from here this morning and fly out later this afternoon."

"Okay. I have work today but not for a few hours." She smiled and climbed on top of him.

Her phone rang on her way home from work, and she smiled at the screen.

"Hi, Mom."

"How was the audition?"

"I got cut before lunch yesterday."

Her mom winced into the phone.

"It's alright. I need to dial back my expectations and work on my stage skills with community theater before I set my sights on regional productions."

"I'm sorry. We're so proud of you for taking the audition, though."

"Thanks, Mom."

"Are you still coming home for St. Patrick's Day?"

"Yep. I'm dating someone new. I'm going to bring him with me."

"Really?" her mom cooed.

"We've dated for a while. I didn't want to say anything in case I jinxed it, but it's going pretty well."

"Tell me all about him."

Penny smiled into the phone and told her mom all about Beckett.

Chapter Eighteen

Guests and bellhops bustled around Beckett in the lobby of the Minneapolis hotel. The board meeting with his new nonprofit ended early. They still couldn't agree on a name, and they needed one soon. The worst part, though, was that the board had voted on a single band for both the dinner portion of the evening and the dancing. They worried that two different entertainers would muddy the wording on the invitation. He hated breaking bad news to people, so he rehearsed how to tell Penny.

He checked his watch. Penny was only ten minutes late. He'd give her another twenty before calling her. Maybe her meeting with the bride about an upcoming wedding gig ran long.

He and Penny had been exclusive for over two months. Penny was nothing like he envisioned, but she was perfect for him. Meeting her family was a big deal, and although he wanted to meet her parents, his stomach soured a bit at the thought of meeting her three older brothers. Penny had explained about the big St. Patrick's day celebration and the activities planned for the weekend, but tonight was for them.

A velvet box sat inside his carry-on luggage. He wanted to give the emerald necklace to her before their dinner reservation. The sound of heels clipping along the marble floor interrupted his thoughts—Penny hustled toward him, pulling her suitcase. Her purse bounced against her hip. He stood to greet her.

"Sorry. The bride and groom couldn't agree on anything. It was a little tense."

"No worries." He kissed her on the cheek. "Our reservation isn't until seven. Let's go up to our suite."

"Great. I need a shower anyway."

He put his hand on her lower back as they made their way to the bank of elevators.

Penny sensed Beckett's irritation as soon as she walked through the hotel doors. He smiled, but his double dimple didn't make an appearance. Even now, alone in the elevator, he kept glancing around instead of looking at her. She pushed the stop button and faced him as the elevator jolted to a halt. "What's wrong?" she asked.

"Why do you think something's wrong?"

"Because you're fake smiling and looking around for an escape hatch."

Beckett sighed. "I'm sorry. My meeting with the nonprofit board didn't go well today. We still don't have a name for the charity, and the fundraiser hit some roadblocks."

"Like what?"

"They voted to only hire one band for the night. I'm sorry,

Penny. I couldn't convince them to hire you to sing during dinner."

He looked like someone had just stolen his last candy bar. Penny squeezed his hand. "It's alright. Don't worry about me. Is that why you're so distracted?"

"Yeah. I didn't know how to tell you."

"It's fine. I'll still go to the event and dance with the man of the hour." She winked at him.

Beckett smiled, and this time his double dimple appeared. "Thanks. They don't know what they're missing." He hit the elevator button.

Penny walked into the suite on the top floor of the hotel. It contained a living area and a separate bedroom. The spa-like bathroom had a walk-in shower and a separate soaking tub. On the coffee table, strawberries and champagne awaited their arrival, and the view out the window of the Mississippi river cut through the city skyline like a ribbon.

Beckett stored their luggage before pulling Penny into his arms.

"We're only here for one night. Why the fancy room?" she asked.

"Because it's been over two months since we started dating, and I wanted you to know how special you are to me."

Her legs trembled—she wrapped her arms around him. What did she do to deserve such love in her life? It was like nothing could ever go wrong. She kissed him and said, "Care to join me in the shower?"

With a reverence usually reserved for fine art, Beckett washed her body and shampooed her curly locks. Every time they were together, she wanted to give more and more of herself to him.

She put in her usual silver hoops and fluffed her hair before dinner. Beckett tied his tie and rustled around in his carry-on. He waited until she applied her lipstick.

"I have something for you," said Beckett.

"You do?"

He nodded. "It's not your birthday or a holiday, but I want you to have this. I love you so much."

Beckett handed her a velvet box, and her hands trembled as she took it. She opened the clasp and gasped—an emerald pendant on a silver chain sat inside. She lifted it out of the box and held it up. He took it from her hand and draped it around her neck. The stone matched her eyes and rested in her cleavage.

"It's gorgeous," she whispered.

"Like you," said Beckett.

"Thank you."

Soft music and the clink of silverware surrounded Penny as she ate her rib eye and mashed potatoes in the upscale restaurant. Beckett ordered a bottle of champagne, and the alcohol relaxed her. Since he was set to meet her family the next day, Penny shared funny stories from her childhood, and Beckett told her stories about Helen during dessert. Penny couldn't remember ever having such a strong connection with another human.

Back in their room, they fell asleep in each other's arms as the day turned over to the next. The silence of her slumber was interrupted by Beckett's jerking body and a shout in his sleep. She opened her eyes and shook him. Was he having a nightmare?

"Beckett? *Beckett.* Wake up. You're dreaming." She shook him until he opened his eyes and gasped for breath. A film of sweat covered his chest—he sat up in bed.

"Sorry, just a dream."

"That wasn't just a dream. It was a nightmare."

"Maybe."

His breath returned to an even cadence. She pulled him under the covers and held him. "What was the nightmare about?"

He threaded his fingers through his hair and closed his eyes. "I don't remember."

She didn't believe him but didn't ask any more questions. Eventually, he drifted back to sleep, but she tossed and turned for hours.

Chapter Nineteen

The next day, Beckett agreed to drive Penny's car to her parents' house in Rochester. She wanted to troll the audition sites on her phone during the drive. She didn't ask any more questions about his nightmare, and he didn't talk about it. He wasn't ready to divulge his role in Helen's death to Penny, yet.

Her car shook and emitted sounds one should never hear from a vehicle. Beckett breathed a sigh of relief when Penny pointed to her driveway in Rochester. It was a minor miracle her car survived the two hours from Minneapolis. Not only that, but the intermittent heat annoyed him, and she needed an oil change.

Beckett turned the car off before facing Penny. "Your car . . ."

"I know, I know. I'll take it in soon. Promise."

They heaved their luggage out of the trunk. Beckett stood in front of Penny's family home—the brick bungalow glowed from light inside the home. The front door opened before they reached the porch. A woman with curly, mid-length, auburn hair opened the door. Penny fell into the woman's arms with a squeal. They clung to each other while Beckett held the bags and straddled the threshold.

"You must be Beckett," said the woman. "Come in, come in. We're so glad you're here."

"Thank you," said Beckett. He set the luggage on the floor and extended his hand to Penny's mother. "It's nice to meet you." Penny's mom laughed. She dismissed his hand and wrapped Beckett in a fierce hug. He initially stiffened in her arms, but he relaxed into the embrace against her soft apron.

"Put your bags in the bedrooms, and come to the kitchen for a chat," said Penny's mom.

Penny led him down a short hallway to a bedroom with a set of bunk beds and one twin bed. A desk sat in the middle of the room, and hockey posters covered the blue walls.

"You'll be in here tonight. I'm next door."

Beckett dropped his bag on the floor of the blue room then followed Penny next door. Boy band posters plastered every inch of her light pink walls. He soaked in the details of her childhood and set her bag on the desk chair. A well-loved, stuffed loon sat on her bed. Framed photos cluttered the top of the dresser, and ribbons and trophies filled the desktop. "Best vocal performance," said Beckett. "Solo and ensemble division one rating. Choral award for best mezzo-soprano. Show choir-Grand Champion."

"Stop. It was high school."

"You were pretty badass in high school," said Beckett.

"I did alright. I had a ton of fun."

He tugged her close and hugged her. "Your mom's nice."

Penny nodded. "She's the best."

Penny led him down the hall and through a living room filled with family photos, framed art from a child's hand, an afghan draped over a couch, and a piano littered with music.

They sat at the kitchen table, and a moment later, her mom set a basket of pretzels on the table and offered them soda.

Penny talked non-stop about her recent audition as her mom measured flour and sugar into a bowl. Beckett ate a pretzel and sipped his soda while the women talked. He noticed more family photos and invitations covering the fridge, while mason jars filled with root sprouts lined the windowsill. A bowl of fruit sat on the edge of the counter, and a pot of coffee warmed on the stove. The low hum of a radio filled the background with noise, and a garbage truck rumbled down their street outside.

It was not unlike Helen's farmhouse on the lake. The memory of playing cards around the scuffed kitchen table with her extended family the day before she died hit him like a punch to the gut.

Penny's mom put something into the oven and carried a large piece of meat from the fridge to the small counter. Penny and her mom volleyed conversation back and forth, catching up on old friends and gossiping about neighbors and acquaintances.

Her dad walked through the door at five o'clock, wearing his electrician's uniform. Beckett stood—Penny's dad was not only taller but broader than him. Beckett straightened his posture and extended his hand.

Penny's dad grasped his hand and met his eyes with warmth.

"Beckett Young."

"Penny tells us you live in Cincinnati but grew up in Boston?"

"Yes, sir."

"Welcome to Rochester. We're glad you're here. I hope the drive was okay."

Penny shot him a pleading look, so he said, "The drive was fine."

Penny's dad moved from the nook to the kitchen and wrapped his wife into his arms. Penny's mom giggled like a schoolgirl, but she leaned into the kiss offered by her husband. The palpable love in the home chewed a giant hole in Beckett's soul. What would it have been like to grow up in a home like Penny's?

Halfway through the meatloaf and tater tot dinner, Penny's mom turned to her and said, "Tell me all about Emma's wedding."

Her dad turned to Beckett while the women lost themselves in wedding details. He asked, "Where do you work in Cincinnati?"

Beckett swallowed his meatloaf and wiped his mouth before facing Penny's dad. "I work for a large PR firm in employee relations. Basically, I onboard new employees to the company."

"Such an important job. I've been with the same company for thirty years. They tried to onboard all their new employees electronically two years ago to save a few bucks. Disaster."

His heart swelled from his comment—Penny's dad had listened to him and found a commonality in their lives. Beckett nodded. "Human connection helps with retention."

"I bet your parents are proud of you."

Beckett was pretty sure his parents didn't even know what he did for a living. They gave up on learning about his professional life when he dismissed their wishes to become an attorney, but he said, "Sure."

After the meal, they divided up tasks. Penny's dad put away the leftovers, and Penny's mom washed the dishes while Beckett dried them. Penny stored the clean dishes in the cabinets and sang a random song while they worked.

Scrabble hit the clean table after Penny's mom removed her apron, and a rousing game began. Penny's mom made popcorn on the stove halfway through the game, and Beckett's stomach ached from laughing at the family stories shared in between turns. Bragging rights went to Penny for the win, and her parents kissed her goodnight before retreating to bed before ten.

When Beckett and Penny were finally alone, they fell into one another on the family room couch. He growled when she pressed against him.

"Shh," said Penny. "Quiet."

"I can be quiet. You're the noisy one."

Penny stifled a laugh and slid her legs across his lap. Later, they retreated to their separate bedrooms. Beckett lay on the skinny twin bed. Although he heard Penny rustling on the other side of the wall, he tamped down his passion for her and turned out the light.

Mass and a parade preceded a family party at the O'Brien home. Beckett filled his plate with corned beef, boiled potatoes, and carrots. He balanced the meal on his knees while sitting on a metal folding chair in the family room. Three broad-shouldered men with varying shades of red hair sauntered toward him. *Uh oh. Here we go.* He set his meal on an end table and stood to face the squad. He stuck his hand out and plastered a smile. The largest of the three shook his hand. "You must be Penny's new boyfriend."

"Beckett Young." He pumped the man's large hand.

"We're Penny's brothers."

"Nice to meet you. I've enjoyed getting to know your parents."

"So, you're serious about our sister?"

"I love Penny."

Two of the brothers inhaled sharply, but before anyone could say another word, a red tornado of curly hair invaded their space. Penny wedged herself in between the men.

"Back off, guys," she said with her hands on her hips.

"Just introducing ourselves," said another of her brothers.

"Yeah, well, I'm a big, grownup girl now," Penny smirked, "And don't need protection anymore, so take your scowling faces somewhere else."

The three hulking men chuckled at Penny and shook Beckett's hand before returning to their families.

"Am I going to get beat up tonight in some dark alley?" asked Beckett as he sat back down with his food on his lap.

Penny grinned. "No. They're huge, but harmless."

The following morning, Beckett drove Penny's car to the Minneapolis airport and ran over a pothole that shook the car like a maraca. "You really should get your car checked out. I can go with you the next time I'm in Misty Lake."

"My car is fine. She shakes and rattles a bit because she's old, and I don't need a man with me to deal with a mechanic."

Beckett pursed his lips. "Fine. I don't have to go, but at least get the oil changed."

"Why are you hounding me about my car? Did my brothers put you up to this?"

"No. But you *should* drive a reliable car."

"This is my car...it's *my* problem."

Beckett huffed. He didn't speak the rest of the way to the airport. When was she going to understand he worried about her because he loved her? He pulled into the departure lane at the Minneapolis airport and retrieved his luggage out of the trunk. Penny popped out of the car to say goodbye. She wrapped her lithe body around his, and he didn't want to let go. He inhaled the scent of her hair and brushed his lips against hers.

"I don't want to fight," said Penny.

"Me either."

"I think the long-distance thing is getting to me."

"Come to Cincinnati for a weekend."

"I can't afford . . ."

"I'll arrange your travel."

Penny's shoulders slumped. "Alright."

Squeaky tennis shoes and the thump of a basketball echoed through the gym of the local Cincinnati Y where Beckett and his buddies played their Saturday morning game against their rival team. The buzzer sounded as Beckett bounced the ball off the backboard and missed the shot. He shook his head and shuffled off the court.

"Sorry, guys, my head's not in the game today." His plan to call his parents after the game hung heavy on his mind—he couldn't focus.

"We'll beat 'em next time." A teammate clapped him on the shoulder.

The guys packed their gym bags and said their goodbyes.

Beckett dragged himself home, showered, cleaned his bathroom, and sorted mail. The necessary call to his mother could wait a little longer. He vacuumed the carpets and under the furniture. He dusted and washed his windows. With his condo clean and nothing else needing his attention, he sank into his couch and dialed his mother.

"Hello, dear."

"Hi, Mom—I mean, Mother. Is Dad home? I need to speak with both of you."

"Your father is traveling."

"Again?"

"Yes. He's an important man with a busy schedule, and I have a spa appointment this afternoon. What can I do for you?" She talked to him like he was on her staff instead of her only child.

He wanted to tell his parents about Penny. He needed them to recant their crazy notion of the list and the trust. "I'm dating a woman."

"Finally. Which girl from the list? I'll call her mother and arrange tea next week."

"She's not on your list."

"Beckett, you can't date any random girl when you should be courting a future spouse from my approved list."

"I met Penny in Minnesota. She's a beautiful, hardworking, talented girl. She's independent and kind. I love her."

His mother sighed. "Well, what does her father do?"

Beckett sidestepped her question. "Penny is an attorney's assistant."

"You're dating a *secretary*?" Beckett held the phone away from his head to protect his ear from her shouting.

"She's also a professional vocalist and auditions for musical theater around the country. Her regular gig is at a bistro on Friday nights." Silence filled the line. "She sings at a church twice a month."

"No, no, *no*. We don't even know where this girl came from. I'm sure there's someone on my list who would suffice."

"I'm dating Penny."

"Unacceptable." The phone clicked off—she'd hung up. Beckett tossed his phone on the coffee table.

. . .

The following Friday, Beckett's knee bounced under his desk at work. The words on the document in front of him were jumbled nonsense. Penny arrived in Cincinnati in twenty-four hours. This time tomorrow, she'd know about the plane and his upscale condo. Would it change her feelings for him? He pushed himself away from his desk and gazed out the window.

Maybe he should tell Penny about his trust and the private jet tonight. He told her he'd arrange for her travel and that her driver would have all the information. Penny agreed. Who wouldn't love a personal ride on a private jet?

Chapter Twenty

On the first Saturday of April, Penny's alarm startled her awake. She'd been dating Beckett since January and was headed to Cincinnati for the first time. Beckett had insisted on securing the flight and didn't want her to miss the plane, so he'd arranged for a driver to take her to the airport at eight in the morning.

A black town car rolled into her drive at seven fifty-eight. A uniformed man opened the back door for her before he took her bag and placed it in the trunk. A uniformed rideshare driver? How weird. He had a jaunty hat and everything. She wanted to snap a picture for a laugh with the girls, but the quiet music and the plush, heated seat soothed her as she settled in for the hundred-mile ride to the Duluth airport. She sipped from her water bottle and relaxed.

Airplanes filled the sky as they closed in on the airport, and Penny reapplied her lipstick. The car exited before the terminal and drove behind an airplane hangar. They pulled up to a small, lone jet sitting on the runway.

"Uh, sir, I think I need to go into the terminal."

"You're flying to Mr. Young, correct?"

"Yes, but what about security?"

"Don't worry ma'am. Mr. Young's plane is perfectly safe."

Mr. Young's plane? What the hell was he talking about? The driver opened her door. She followed him and her suitcase up the stairs and inside the airplane. A flight attendant greeted her at the top of the stairs and accepted the luggage from the driver.

"Welcome, Miss O'Brien. Please choose any seat. I'll be with you in a moment."

How did the flight attendant know her name? Penny swung her head from side to side. The taupe leather seats were in different arrangements. A few seats surrounded tables, and there were two together like a bench. Penny sat facing forward in a regular seat, and her body molded into the squishy leather. Dirty, hard seats and passengers crammed into tiny spaces on commercial flights paled in comparison to this plane. She pulled out her phone and texted Beckett. *Holy shit. A private plane?*

Beckett texted back. *You deserve the best. Enjoy your flight. Can't wait to see you. Love you.*

Why didn't he tell her about the plane ahead of time? Beckett had money—maybe even a lot of money—but paying for an expensive dinner and buying a piece of jewelry were completely different from owning a private jet. What else didn't she know about him? Penny buckled her seat belt and picked at her thumbnail until the flight attendant came to her seat.

"Can I get you something to drink? Water, juice, coffee? Mr. Young requested you be served a light snack for the early morning flight. Would you prefer a bagel or a scone with the fruit plate?" The flight attendant placed a pillow and fleece blanket on the seat beside her.

"Um, thank you."

"A bagel or scone, Miss O'Brien?"

"A scone, please."

"Anything to drink?"

"Coffee?"

"I'll be back with your order after take-off."

The plane sped down the runway and lifted into the clouds. Her belly lurched, and her ears plugged. She swallowed and slowed her breaths. Once the plane leveled off, the flight attendant arrived with coffee, scones, and a fruit plate.

"Thank you." Penny sipped the coffee and let the hot, rich aroma settle her nerves. The quiet flight ended with a gentle bump on the runway before they taxied away from the other commercial airlines. She peered through the window and saw Beckett leaning against a car beside a hangar. His arms were folded against his leather jacket, and his aviator sunglasses hid his eyes. Another new jacket? His hair blew in the breeze. He smiled and removed his sunglasses when the plane stopped.

"Thank you for flying with us," said the flight attendant as Penny walked down the stairs to the tarmac. "We'll see you tomorrow evening."

Beckett opened his arms to her, but she stopped short of them. He put his arms down as she folded hers. "A private plane? How come you didn't tell me? How do you even own a private jet?"

Beckett shifted on his feet and cast a look at the crew, who were eyeing him with worried expressions. He waved and smiled at them before returning his attention to Penny. "It's the family plane. A hand-me-down."

"I don't think you know what hand-me-down means," Penny muttered.

"My surprises aren't working very well with you. C'mon. Let's go to my house."

He took Penny's bag and set it in the trunk. Penny sat in the passenger seat of the Jaguar and stretched her legs in the classy car. She was pretty sure the interior of the car had more square feet than her bathroom.

The outside sounds silenced, and Beckett merged into traffic. He pointed out various landmarks along the way. After a twenty-minute drive, he pulled into an underground garage downtown. They rode an elevator up to the fifteenth floor, and the doors swished open to his condo. The elevator opened to his house? Did he own the whole floor? Her pulse raced as she followed Beckett inside. Sun splashed through the floor-to-ceiling windows, bathing the living area in natural light. His spotless gourmet kitchen with high-end appliances and smooth counters was three times the size of her mom's kitchen. She counted four doors down a long hall. "You live here by yourself?"

"Yeah. It's close to work." She followed him down the hall to his bedroom. A fluffy, gray down duvet and navy-blue pillows covered a king-size sleigh bed. She ran her hand over the smooth wood and along the soft linens.

"I need to check on lunch. Come on out after you freshen up," said Beckett.

The view from the picture window included the skyline and a park below. The drapes framing the large window matched the pillows on the bed. She walked across the room and bent down to sniff the fresh daisies in a crystal vase on the dresser. Then she set her bag at the foot of the bed and found the door to the primary bathroom. It contained a full vanity with two sinks and a separate shower and soaking tub. Geez. Her entire apartment would fit in Beckett's bathroom.

HR jobs didn't make *that* much money, did they? She sat on the edge of the bed and twisted her hands. Mark and Emma were older than Beckett, and they both worked. Their home was nice but nothing like Beckett's condo. And the luxury car? The plane? What the hell? Her stomach dropped. What didn't she know about him? Was he a drug dealer? A gambler with good luck? Part of a crime family?

She joined Beckett in the kitchen, where he spooned minestrone soup into bowls and set them on the table with bread and salad.

"I thought we could eat lunch here and go out to dinner?"

"Um, sure." She picked at her food and ate a few bites of the flavorful soup.

Beckett put his spoon down. "What's wrong? Are you mad about the plane?"

"No. Yes. I don't know." She set her spoon down. "It's everything—your condo, the plane, the Jag, and the expensive dinners and the jewelry, and exactly how many coats do you own?"

"My coats? What's wrong with my jackets?"

"Nothing, but you have so many. And your condo—it's *huge*. You don't even share the floor with anyone else."

"It's my house."

"But your furniture is real and stuff. My nightstand is a crate from the supermarket."

"I'm older than you, and I've worked longer."

Penny shook her head. "What else?"

Beckett sat back in his chair. "My parents have a little money. I bought the condo and car with part of my trust fund."

Penny exhaled. "So, you're not a gambler or a drug dealer?"

"No."

"You're not part of a crime family?"

"Nothing illegal going on here. Just a boring trust fund."

"And the trust fund paid for the plane and private drivers?"

"Sure."

"The Jag?"

"I guess so."

Penny's stomach unclenched. She ate a spoonful of the soup and scanned the main living area. A huge Michigan flag hung over the TV—at least that was normal. "Why didn't you tell me about the plane?"

"Because I wanted you to love me for me...not my money."

Penny thought about his statement. Most of the guys she had dated had about as much money as her, so wealth never factored into her relationships. Maybe it did for other women, though. "I'm sorry I was angry when I got off the plane. I couldn't figure out why you didn't tell me, and my imagination went wild."

Beckett squeezed her hand. "It's okay. I get why you were mad. I should've told you. Come on, let's eat. I want to show you the riverwalk."

In the afternoon, they basked in the early spring sunshine along the river. Beckett pointed out the building where he worked and the Y where he played basketball with his buddies. She pushed the trust fund and plane to the back of her brain and focused on the man who loved the University of Michigan, basketball...and her.

They clutched gloved hands and stole kisses on the way back to his condo. Beckett hung their coats, and Penny wandered around his living room. The late afternoon sun streamed through his windows and warmed the space. Penny soaked up the view of the other skyscrapers and river in the distance. Beckett wrapped his arms around her, and she leaned her head back on his shoulder.

"I don't want to go to some fancy restaurant and pretend to like food I don't recognize. Let's order in for dinner," said Penny.

Beckett smiled. "Great idea."

"Pizza and a movie?"

"Perfect."

Penny dismissed the new information about Beckett, and they split a pizza and drank beer on his couch. They laughed through a rom-com and focused on each other the rest of the night.

Her eyes blinked open the next morning as Beckett turned onto his back and flopped a hand above his head, still asleep. She turned on her side and marveled at the man beside her. She loved his generosity and kindness, along with his unruly hair and clear blue eyes. He supported her dream and encouraged her. Their financial differences were bigger than she thought, but he didn't dwell on it. She loved that he was happy to hang out and watch a movie at home instead of impressing her at a fancy restaurant. He worshiped her body and accepted her desire to wait for sex without question or pressure. Was she ready to lose her virginity to him? She had waited for love, and Beckett was her first true love. Her sex pulsed. She couldn't wait for him to wake up.

Beckett snored for another hour. Penny sighed and leaned over to help him along. She brushed her lips against his smooth chest and inhaled his scent. Her hand trailed down his stomach, around the curve of his hip, and onto his strong thigh. His cock twitched, and she kissed his pecs and neck. He smiled with his eyes closed and wrapped an arm around her.

He tugged her close. "Hmm. Now, that's a great way to wake up."

Penny kissed him on the lips and whispered, "I'm ready."

He kissed her back. "Ready for what?"

"You."

"You've got me."

"No. I'm ready. Make love to me."

Beckett's eyes flew open. "What?"

"I love you. I love you more than coffee and singing and loons. Make love to me."

Beckett turned and faced her, now fully awake. "You sure?"

She nodded.

"Positive?"

"Yes."

Beckett flipped her onto her back and spent the next hour pleasuring her with his hands and mouth. After rocking her world twice, she yanked him back up her body and said, "Beckett, please."

He pulled open his bedside table drawer and grabbed a condom. Her pulse ratcheted up, and her belly turned somersaults. He centered his body over her, and his eyes never strayed from hers. She gripped his hips as a flash of white-hot pain seared through her core.

Beckett stopped moving. "Are you alright?" he asked.

Penny's muscles relaxed. "Never better."

Beckett kissed her lips, and when he moved again, Penny moved with him.

Chapter Twenty-One

On Sunday night, after the most sensual encounter of his life, Beckett drove Penny back to the airport. Making love with Penny was as close as he'd ever been to a spiritual experience. Their bodies and souls had entwined and moved together as one. He loved her more than he'd ever loved anyone in his whole life, and he didn't want to spend a minute without her.

"We need to go on a trip in the Boundary Waters," said Penny. "You should experience what the kids will do when they receive their scholarships."

Beckett merged off the interstate and onto the airport exit. His stomach soured. The last place he wanted to be was on a lake in the Boundary Waters.

"It'll be great," she continued. "We'll have Mark map out an easy trip, and I can teach you how to portage over the lakes. I'll show you how to build a campfire and pitch a tent. Sleeping in the woods is the best."

"I don't know. I'm not the camping type. I'm more of a hotel and restaurant kind of guy."

Penny snorted. "Yeah, I know. But it'll take my mind off my auditions. How about the first weekend in May?"

"So soon? Are you sure?"

"Well, one of these days, I'm gonna land a part on the stage, and I'll be tied up for months."

"Okay."

Beckett pulled up next to his plane and faced Penny. "I had the best weekend."

"Me, too. I love you."

"I love you." He kissed her long and hard before sending her off. His plane flew her up into the sky.

Back in his condo, Beckett opened his computer and clicked on a camping store site. He didn't have a clue what to bring or wear on a canoe camping trip. What if something happened? He could fly her anywhere in the world, but she wanted to drag him canoe camping in the Boundary Waters. His phone rang, and he swiped without looking at the name on the screen.

"You need to mark a date on your calendar," said his mother.

He winced at the sound of her voice. "What for, Mother?"

"We're expected to be at Goldman's fortieth anniversary party in June. They're our oldest and dearest friends, and they want you to attend. I'll secure a suitable escort for you."

"No. Penny will be my date."

"Who's Penny?"

Beckett blew out a breath. "The woman I've dated since the New Year."

"The bar singer you told me about? No, no, no. Not at a high society party, dear. She'll embarrass us."

"I won't go without Penny."

"What's the point? You're not going to marry her."

"Who says I won't marry her?" Beckett challenged his mother. He waited for his mother's retort, but he broke the silence on the line. "I'm in love with Penny."

"Beckett, you know the rules. You marry a girl from the list, or you lose your trust."

"I won't be at the party without Penny."

Silence filled the line.

"Mother?"

"Why are you doing this to me?" she whispered into the phone before she hung up.

* * *

On Beckett's plane back to Minnesota, Penny shifted in her seat. The soreness from a whole day of lovemaking gave way to a dull ache on the long flight, but she couldn't imagine a bond stronger than the one she shared with Beckett. The pulse of another human inside her body filled her with wonder. When he came inside of her for the first time, they shared tears of joy from the intimate moment.

The rest of their day together was spent murmuring and kissing in between their lovemaking. She couldn't imagine a more perfect way to express her love to Beckett and didn't feel whole without him beside her. As the plane began its descent, she willed herself to focus on her next audition.

A small theater north of Minneapolis opened auditions for *Annie.* In the weeks following her trip to Cincinnati, Penny rehearsed choreography and sang in the music room at the church every night after work. She lived and breathed the audition repertoire. Her skills improved after the disaster in Cleveland, and her confidence soared. Her audition for a minor role went a thousand times better than the one in Cleveland, but by the end of the first day, the director cut her from the cast.

She pushed through the rejection and packed for her weekend in the Boundary Waters with Beckett. The bugs wouldn't be awful, and the water would be chilly, but it would take her mind off the rejections. Beckett kept trying to beg off the trip, but he finally agreed to meet her at Mark's Gere the following weekend.

Chapter Twenty-Two

Patchy fog swirled around Beckett's jet as it landed at the Duluth airport on the first Saturday in May for the canoe camping trip in the Boundary Waters. Penny had asked him to meet her at Mark's outfitter store, and the plan was to 'put in' on the lake behind the store. As he rounded the corner of the outfitter store two hours later, he found Mark tidying a pile of camping gear by the back door as Penny checked items off a list. Penny looked up at Beckett as he approached and swiftly swallowed a giggle, but Mark laughed out loud.

"What?" Beckett asked. He glanced down, taking stock of his gear: he had bought new hiking boots, a flannel shirt, some sort of important base layer, hiking pants, and a designer vest with a million pockets. A compass and pocket knife hung from a carabiner on his belt. Was he missing something?

"Hey, man, did a camping store throw up on you?" asked Mark.

"I've never been camping, so I went to a store and asked the salesman for advice."

"Did you buy the whole store?" asked Penny.

"Sorta," Beckett admitted.

"Rule number one: No one cares what you look or smell like," said Penny. She stood before him in a long-sleeve T-shirt and a pair of jeans with holes in the knees.

"Okay, okay. Fine. Let's go," said Beckett.

Mark handed them life jackets, and Penny double checked the list.

"I'll teach you how to paddle, first," said Penny.

Beckett clipped his life jacket, tightened the straps, checked the clips again, and patted his life vest.

"Did you hear me?" asked Penny.

"Sorry. Just making sure the life jacket is secure."

"It's fine. Here." She handed him a canoe paddle. "We're going to practice paddling on land before we get into the water."

Beckett sighed, relieved. Paddling on land sounded much safer than anything in the water.

After Penny taught Beckett how to paddle, he practiced by the shore of the lake while she and Mark organized the gear in the canoe. Fifteen minutes later, Penny instructed him to sit in the front of the canoe while she hopped into the back. The canoe rocked a bit when she got in, and Beckett gripped the sides.

Mark shoved the canoe into the lake, and before Beckett blinked, they were in the water. Beckett dipped his paddle into the lake—he didn't realize how close to the water's surface they'd be. The only other boat he'd been on in his life was a cruise ship, and the water was six floors below. He checked his life jacket clips again and cinched the straps even tighter across his chest.

"You alright?" Penny called from the back of the canoe.

"Fine."

"We're going to be here for days unless you help me paddle."

He turned around to Penny, and she winked at him before pulling her paddle through the clear water.

"Sorry." Beckett paddled from the bow. His arms pulled the paddle through the water like Penny had taught him, but water splashed into the canoe and got his pants wet. He found a rhythm after a while, though grimaced when his arms burned from the strain.

Penny steered them across the small lake and slowed the canoe by the shore. His shoulders relaxed when the canoe bumped onto dry land.

"Are we done?"

Penny laughed. "No. This is our first portage."

"What's a portage?"

"We need to carry the canoe and all the stuff to the next lake."

"Another lake?"

"Yeah. Come on. Grab some gear and set it on the rocks. I'll carry the canoe." Beckett stepped into the six inches of water and onto the shore. He helped Penny unload the packs and tent, then held the canoe as she ducked under it and lifted it.

When she walked up the trail with the canoe balanced on her shoulders, Beckett whistled low. "Damn." He followed her up the trail with a pack on his back and the tent in his arms.

They made one trip back to the portage entrance to retrieve the rest of their gear then loaded everything back into the hull of the canoe. His heart beat hard when he saw the huge lake in front of them—he couldn't even see the other side.

"Are we going across the whole thing?" He couldn't imagine how deep it was in the middle. They were going to die for sure.

Penny referenced her map. "Mark reserved a campsite for

us on the west side of the lake. A couple of hours or so of paddling. Easy day."

They pushed the canoe into the bigger lake, and Beckett tightened his life jacket straps and pulled his paddle through the water. After a while, he relaxed—at least a little bit. He even dared to look around at the scenery as they rounded an island, heading west on the lake.

"Look," said Penny. "Loons." She pointed in the direction where two loons swam in the lake. Their tremolo call sounded over the water.

"They're laughing at us," said Beckett.

"Nah. It's the call they make when they're feeling threatened. They don't like us being so close."

"Do they always stick together?" asked Beckett.

"Loons have one mate at a time. They can get separated, so they don't necessarily mate for life, but when they're together on the lake, they're exclusive—like us. A couple of loons in love."

After another hour of paddling, a campsite surrounded by tall birch trees came into view. A fire grate sat in the middle of the site. Behind it, there was a grassy area for the tent. They grounded the canoe on the sandy beach and stepped out. Beckett gave a small prayer of thanks for dry land and the latrine he spotted behind the campsite. He helped Penny pitch the tent before they walked into the forest to collect firewood. Once Penny built the fire and tied down the canoe, they sat on a log.

Beckett poked at the fire while she prepped dinner. "Wow. Canoe camping is a lot of work."

Penny stirred the pot of freeze-dried food. "Yep, and look at the reward." She waved her hand toward the lake. "Open water, sunshine, and endless beauty. My first Boundary Waters trip was with Northern Woods two summers ago. I knew how to camp, but tripping from lake to lake was new to me."

"We camped for our family vacation every summer," Penny continued. "My poor mom must have spent weeks preparing a family of six for camping in the wilderness, but I got to play in the woods, and my dad fished. My brothers messed around in the lake, and we all sang around the campfire at night. I think canoe camping through the Boundary Waters would've pushed my mom over the edge, but my dad would've loved it."

"Your parents are awesome. How long have they been married?"

"Thirtyish years, why?"

"They're still in love."

Penny wrinkled her nose. "I know. They were so embarrassing in high school. I bet your parents are well-behaved."

Beckett shifted on the log and folded his hands on his knees. "My mother called the other night. I've been invited to an anniversary party in June, and I'd like you to be my date. Their friends are celebrating their fortieth. It'll be a formal affair."

Penny grabbed his arm and smiled wide. "I'd love to go. I can't wait to meet your parents. All my ex-boyfriends' parents loved me. Never failed. I still keep in touch with one mom but haven't talked to her son in like five years."

"Are you sure? Because I'll understand if you don't want to go."

"Don't be silly. It'll be great."

She ladled the dinner into bowls. Taking his bowl, he blew on a spoonful. After he swallowed the bland mixture, he said, "My mother and father are different from yours."

"How?"

"More formal."

"Well, they have staff to do the boring stuff like take out the trash, so they must channel their energy on the more formal stuff."

Beckett stared at Penny. He didn't know what to say. Should he tell her their only passion was money? That their friends thought they lived a glamorous life when, in fact, there was no love in the house? Should he tell her his mother had a list of potential women for him to marry, and if he strayed off the list, he'd lose his trust?

A mosquito buzzed around her forehead. "Eat up. The skeeters are out for their dinner."

They washed the dishes, then Penny taught him how to hang the food bag so it didn't attract bears. *Bears? Was she kidding?* Penny extinguished the fire before they scrambled into the tent.

"Whew," said Penny. She fished a travel-sized tent light out of her pack and illuminated the small space. She pulled out her sleeping bag, zipped it all the way open, and spread it on the tent floor. After they zipped Beckett's sleeping bag onto Penny's, they lay on their sides facing one another. They talked for a long time, but Beckett was too cowardly to confess any of his family's dysfunction. A wailing call pierced the night.

"A loon?" asked Beckett.

"Yep."

"It sounds different from earlier on the lake."

"Loons have a bunch of different calls. The wailing call is when a loon has lost their mate or chicks. A lonely loon is the saddest sound in the world."

The wailing in the distance persisted, and Beckett pulled Penny against himself as they drifted off to sleep. By morning, Penny had spooned into his chest and legs. He ran a hand along her hip. Sun streamed into the tent, and she rolled over.

"Morning," said Beckett.

"Isn't sleeping in the woods awesome?"

"The dark is nice. Do you ever get used to all the noises from the birds and the bugs?"

"Not really."

Penny moved her hand up to his face and ran a finger along his stubble. When she cupped his chin, her soft skin sent shivers up his spine. She pressed her lips to his. The kiss deepened, but when he shifted, he felt a sharp edge.

"Aagh," Beckett yelped. "I could do without the sticks digging into my back."

Penny laughed as she got up. She unzipped the tent and left to use the latrine.

They hiked in the woods after breakfast. Thrilled to be out of the water, he asked her a million questions about hiking and camping in general. She helped him identify poison ivy and explained what to do if they ran into a bear. Afterwards, they rounded a corner on the trail and took a break on a log.

"I need a name for the nonprofit," said Beckett. "The invitations for the gala fundraiser go out soon, and they can't be delivered without a name."

"Hmm. Let's brainstorm. How about Helen's Kids," said Penny.

"Canoes for kids," said Beckett.

"Paddling for all."

"Learn the Lakes."

"Paddle Pals."

"Boundless Adventures."

They sat silent for a while and thought. "Ripple Effects," said Penny.

He smiled at her. "Perfect." He wrapped an arm around her shoulders and gave her a tender kiss. *Ripple Effects* was the ideal name for the nonprofit. Helen didn't want money to

prevent any child from experiencing the Boundary Waters—
donations would enable children of all ages and backgrounds to
experience the adventure of a lifetime. Helen believed any
child who encountered nature at a young age would appreciate
it for life and share it with others. A true ripple effect.

After lunch, the sun beat down on them as they sat on the
beach and talked. Penny dipped her toes into the water. "This
cove is pretty shallow and not too chilly. Let's go for a swim."
She whipped off her top and stood to pull down her shorts. "I
can't stand to be near water and not be in it."

His heart skipped several beats, blood draining from his
face. "But we don't have swim suits," said Beckett, watching
Penny toss her clothes into a messy pile on the beach. She
flipped her hair and made a bun on top of her head.

"We don't need swimsuits." She unhooked her bra and
shimmied out of her underwear before toeing naked into the
lake.

"Come on, it's not too cold," said Penny.

Beckett stood on the beach as Penny jogged through the
shallow lake. She dove under the water—his body shook,
muscles tightening. He couldn't breathe. "No...No...Stop!" He
yelled. Where was she? The water splashed, but she was too far
away—he couldn't see her. "Come back! Penny! No! Penny?
Come back!"

* * *

The cold water sluiced across her naked body. She shivered,
and goosebumps covered her skin. The deeper she swam, the
colder the water became, but there was nothing better than
swimming in the Boundary Waters—a quick dip wouldn't hurt,

and the sun was warm. A fish swam under her as she dove down to get a closer look at a pretty rock.

She'd heard Beckett shouting something from the beach before she pierced the water's surface, but she couldn't hear him now. He better join her soon.

She treaded the water and looked around. "Shit, shit, shit." She saw Beckett on his knees on the beach, holding his head in his hands. Penny swam as hard as she could and ran out of the lake, ignoring the sting of the sharp rocks on her feet.

She knelt down beside him, water dripping onto his clothes. "Beckett? Beckett! What's wrong?" She pushed him to sit, and his whole body shook like a frightened dog during a thunderstorm. He sobbed into his hands, but Penny couldn't figure out what happened—he was fine two minutes ago.

"You're okay?" Beckett asked in between the sobs wracking his body.

"A little chilly but fine. What's wrong?"

He cried onto her shoulder.

Penny waited until his sobs became hiccups. "Hold on. I need some clothes. The water was colder than I thought." She grabbed her underwear and slipped them over her wet, sand-encrusted thighs. She pulled her T-shirt on, covering her bare breasts. "What's going on?"

Beckett breathed and wiped his face with his T-shirt. "Helen died because of me."

Penny inhaled a sharp breath but rested her hand on Beckett's back. "Tell me what happened."

"Helen invited me to her lake house for a weekend last August. All of her kids and grandchildren were there. There were boat rides and games during the day on Saturday. We ate tons of food and built a bonfire in the evening. The kids ran around catching fireflies and making s'mores. The adults drank beer and talked. It was a late night." Penny rubbed his back as he took another shaky breath.

"I fell asleep as soon as I hit the bed, but the sun woke me up early the next morning. The old farmhouse doesn't have air conditioning—the bedroom was stuffy. I needed some fresh air. And it was so nice and quiet with the kids still asleep, so—so I poured a cup of coffee. I was on the back porch—" Beckett paused and sniffled. "—Helen was standing on the dock. I saw her putting on her swim cap and goggles. She never missed a day when the lake wasn't frozen."

Beckett stifled another sob. Penny couldn't imagine where his story was going, but she picked up his hand and said, "It's me. You can tell me."

"I sat in my favorite rocking chair on the porch, and Helen turned around and waved at me. I held up my coffee cup in salute. She dove into the water and swam a steady stroke toward the other side of the lake. She turned around to head back and then . . ."

"Then what?" asked Penny.

Beckett sniffled. "She vanished in the murky water. I waited, but there were no more splashes. When she didn't surface, I ran off the porch and waded into the water as far as I could go, and I screamed her name a hundred times, and—" Beckett wiped more tears, "—the noise of my yelling woke her kids. I dialed 911. I stood in chest-deep water and pointed as her children dove off the dock and swam past me to find her. I couldn't save her because...because . . ."

"Because what?" Penny asked.

". . . I couldn't swim."

Chapter Twenty-Three

A MILLION THOUGHTS ran through Penny's mind. Why did Helen go under? Did Helen's kids find her? Why couldn't Beckett swim? Did they try to revive her? What did Beckett do? Helen was a strong swimmer, so something must've happened while she was under the water. Penny wanted to pepper Beckett with questions, but she rubbed his back and let him continue.

"Firemen splashed by me in the lake. Helen's son pulled her from the water and dragged her to the shore on the other side of the lake. He performed CPR. It was awful. I backed out of the water and collapsed on the lawn. Her grandchildren huddled on the porch, and I couldn't even look at them. A cop asked me for my statement, and I told him Helen swam one length of the lake, turned around, and disappeared. I told him I couldn't swim, so I couldn't rescue her."

Beckett turned and faced Penny. "When you jumped in the lake and swam away from me, I lost it."

The lake lapped at the beach, and Penny envisioned the scene at the farmhouse. Helen could've hit her head on the turnaround or got her foot caught in something under the water. A seizure or stroke in the lake would render her helpless. "Do you even know how she died?" she asked Beckett.

Beckett nodded. "The autopsy revealed Helen died of a heart attack while swimming in the lake. But if I'd been able to swim, I could've helped her."

"Not necessarily."

Beckett hung his head. "I know. The docs said the heart attack was massive, and my cousins don't blame me, but the guilt overwhelmed me at the beginning."

"Helen had a bad heart. You probably couldn't have saved her even if you could swim."

"Maybe, but I didn't even try. I was helpless."

It never even occurred to her to ask Beckett if he could swim when she planned their trip. She dragged him into the Boundary Waters even though he'd begged to call off the trip a dozen times over the past two weeks. "Can you swim now?"

"A little. I signed up for private lessons at the Y last fall. I know the basics, but I couldn't save you if something happened while you were swimming in this lake."

"Your panic attack makes sense now. Why didn't you tell me?"

"I was embarrassed. I mean, who doesn't know how to swim? I'm sorry. I should've told you."

"We already have the challenge of a long-distance relationship. Withholding stuff from each other just makes it tougher."

Beckett nodded.

"Let's eat an early dinner. A storm is on the horizon."

A weight lifted off Beckett's shoulders after he told Penny the story of Helen's accident. She listened and didn't judge him.

They talked about his guilt and the nightmares following the accident. He told her how working on the nonprofit and their relationship helped him heal.

A cold drizzle dampened their evening, and the sky darkened before dinner. Penny cooked supper, and when the winds picked up, she asked Beckett to tie the tent fly down in case of a storm. After dishes, she secured the canoe and paddles by the lakeshore. Darkness came early, and rumbles of thunder sounded in the distance. They lay in their sleeping bag and counted in between the flashes of lightning and thunder to estimate the distance of the storm. Rain and wind lashed the tent, and a puddle formed in one corner. They clung to each other through the night and fell asleep when the storm quieted.

Penny and Beckett packed up their gear after a soggy breakfast the next morning. Penny checked his life jacket before they boarded the canoe. Conversation was minimal until they reached the shore where Mark met them and helped sort the gear on the lawn. When everything was stored, Beckett held Penny in the parking lot.

"I'll send the plane to you in three weeks for the anniversary party. We'll buy a gown for you in Cincinnati."

Penny nuzzled his chest. "Alright. Don't worry. The next trip won't be stressful at all. Meeting the parents is easy." She kissed him.

Beckett returned her kiss, but dread filled his soul. He'd never introduced a woman to his parents, but he knew it wouldn't be easy.

Chapter Twenty-Four

In a boutique dress shop in downtown Cincinnati, Beckett sat on a pink wingback chair as Penny twirled in gowns of red, green, pale pink, black, and navy blue. The anniversary party required a formal gown, and the activity took his mind off their impending trip to Boston.

"They're all beautiful, pick one."

"Are you sure I need a long gown?"

"The invitation is black tie. I'll be in a tux."

Penny disappeared into the dressing room. Moments later, she emerged in the dark blue gown. She spun around. "I like the neckline, and the spaghetti straps will support the girls."

"There you go, win, win."

They grabbed lunch at a brew pub in the city and finished their day at the lingerie store. Beckett picked out teddies, baby-dolls, silk nighties, and bras of every color before Penny dragged him out of the store.

"I'll never be able to wear all of this stuff."

"You're right. I like you best naked, anyways."

• • •

Two days later, Beckett's stomach clenched when the airport came into view. The driver pulled up next to his plane, and Penny bounded up the stairs. She hugged and chatted with his flight attendant like they'd been friends forever.

Beckett picked at the snack the flight attendant brought them. He still hadn't gotten up the courage to tell Penny much about his family. He convinced himself there was no way to prepare Penny for his parents. How could he tell her his mother didn't know what he did for a living? Or that her life revolved around society functions and not her family? Should he tell Penny he didn't think his parents ever loved each other... or him?

Instead of delving into the messiness of his family life, he sat silent on the plane. His stomach lurched when they hit a patch of turbulence, and he asked the flight attendant to remove his food.

Penny touched his hand. "What's wrong?"

Beckett slumped in his seat. He had to tell her something. "My parents. They're not like your parents. They, um...have different priorities."

"Like what?"

"Money and social status."

"Oh."

"And they're not very affectionate." Doubt and confusion clouded Penny's face. He clasped her hand. "Whatever happens, remember, I love you."

The last hour of the flight was smooth, and they landed in Boston in the mid-afternoon. Beckett clasped Penny's hand down the plane's stairs but dropped it to bear hug Jackson. He held on, slapping him on the shoulder when they parted. "Lookin' good, Jackson. Thanks for meeting us. I'd like you to meet my girlfriend, Penny."

Jackson tipped his hat and smiled widely. "Miss Penny, a

pleasure to meet you. Any friend of Mister Young's is a friend of mine."

"Mr. Jackson, thank you. I'm so excited to be here. I've never been to Boston."

Jackson loaded the luggage into the trunk and opened the door for Penny and Beckett. After they slid in the back seat, Jackson drove off the tarmac.

* * *

Penny settled into the plush seats of the car, and the city raced by through the window. Jackson and Beckett talked about basketball and the summer tourist season on the coast. After an hour-long ride through thick traffic, Jackson slowed the car and pulled up to a wrought-iron ornamental gate that opened slowly by itself. They drove through, continuing uphill along a winding road until an estate came into view. A massive, white structure stood on top of a cliff, and the ocean sparkled in the distance. A uniformed man opened the car door, greeting them after they'd parked in the circle drive.

Penny stepped onto the drive with her purse while Jackson unloaded the trunk. She ran around to the back of the car and pulled the handle up on her luggage. She walked with it for about two feet until a deep voice said, "I'll take this, miss." The uniformed man took her suitcase and everything else from the trunk before whisking it all away.

Beckett grabbed her hand.

"Your parents have staff to haul the luggage?" Penny whispered.

Beckett nodded.

Penny stood back and surveyed the massive building in front of her. Four large columns flanked a double wide entry door, and pots full of colorful flowers lined the entryway.

Dozens of windows reflected a manicured lawn with nary a blade out of line, and she itched to touch the grass to see if it was real.

Penny swung her huge purse over her shoulder and held Beckett's hand as another man opened the door for them, inviting them to enter the home. An enormous chandelier lit the two-story entryway, and fresh floral arrangements covered tables. Penny's low-heeled sandals clicked on the marble floor as they walked down the hall past a large sitting room, ballroom, and office space. The wide hall gave way to a circular staircase, and a wave of nausea rolled over Penny. She clutched her stomach.

Beckett stopped. "Penny?"

"I don't belong here," Penny whispered. "My parents' entire home would fit in this foyer."

Beckett squeezed her hand. "You belong here because you're with me."

"What if I break something?"

"You won't break anything, and if you did, it wouldn't matter. C'mon, let's find Mother."

Beckett turned a corner, and Penny lost track of where they were in the house. They walked down another long hallway to a room with more furniture than the entirety of her parents' house. Penny's eyes trailed to the high ceilings. How did they get the cobwebs out of the corners?

When she stole a glance at Beckett, she noticed a thin line of sweat beading his upper lip. She questioned him with her eyes, but he shook his head. They approached a thin, blonde woman in a royal blue linen suit and heels. The afternoon sun streamed through the floor-to-ceiling windows, making the diamonds at her throat sparkle. A crystal glass filled with brown liquid sat on the table beside her. His mother's pursed lips hid her smile.

"Mother, how're you today?" Beckett bent and kissed the air beside her cheek.

"The service omitted foie gras from the delivery, but I corrected the error. It's so difficult to find decent staff these days."

"Wouldn't want to be without duck liver." Beckett mumbled. He cleared his throat. "Mother, I'd like to introduce you to my girlfriend. Penny, my mother."

Penny stepped toward the woman and held out her hand. "Mrs. Young, it's so great to meet you." The woman barely grazed Penny's fingers with her own—hardly a handshake—and surveyed her from head to toe like a mannequin in a department store. Penny remembered Beckett saying his parents weren't affectionate, but the woman glared at her. "Oh! I almost forgot. I have something for you."

"You do?" said Beckett.

"Yeah. Hold on. Let me find it. My bag swallows everything." She rustled around in her purse and came up with a small box wrapped in black paper, finished with a white bow. She handed it to Beckett's mother. Beckett wrapped his arm around Penny's waist.

Mrs. Young untied the ribbon and set it on the table beside her drink. She removed the wrapping paper and stared at the wooden box.

"Um...thank you." She turned it over and around in her hands.

"It's a jewelry box with a loon on the front," said Penny. "The loon is Minnesota's state bird. They're beautiful creatures, right, Beckett?"

"Amazing birds. Wasn't it thoughtful of Penny to bring you a gift, Mother?"

Beckett's mother screwed up her lips and turned her glare on Beckett.

Mrs. Young set the wooden box down on the table. Silence filled the room.

Penny said to Beckett, "I'd love to see the rest of the house."

"Let's go."

"See ya later, Mrs. Young."

Penny held the railing as they walked up the wide stairs and down another hallway. Beckett led her into a room with a four-poster bed, reading nook, and attached bathroom. The pale peach linens complimented the fabrics of the furniture, and landscape portraits of the ocean graced the walls. The room resembled a hotel suite rather than a bedroom in a home. Her luggage sat at the foot of the bed. She sank on the edge of the bed and tilted her head to meet Beckett's eyes. "Well, your mother didn't like me."

Beckett shrugged his shoulders.

"When did you last see her?"

"Six months ago, at Christmas."

"You didn't hug her hello."

He sighed. "I told you, my parents aren't affectionate."

"But you did hug Jackson."

"I love Jackson."

Penny frowned and put her hand on Beckett's arm. "Talk to me."

Beckett sat on the bed beside Penny and rested his elbows on his thighs. "My relationship with my parents is complicated. I grew up with a nanny who taught me how to do things like tie my shoes and zip my jacket. Jackson helped me with the big stuff—girls and driving. My mother and father were always busy with important events for my dad's work or social functions with their friends."

A knock at the door interrupted them. A maid said to Beckett, "Mrs. Young would like to see you in the drawing room."

"Tell her I'll be right there." To Penny, he said, "I'll go find out what Mother wants, and I'll be right back." He left and closed the door.

* * *

Beckett returned to the drawing room. "What's up?"

"Don't 'what's up' me. Sit."

Beckett stood and crossed his arms over his chest. His mother sipped her drink and folded her hands. "Your girlfriend is pretty," said his mother.

Beckett smiled, and the pounding in his head lessened. "You should hear her sing. She's amazing."

His mother shook her head. "Dear, she's a nice, short-term plaything for you, but you can't be serious about her."

"I'm in love with her."

His mother rolled her eyes. "She gave me a wooden box with a duck on the front, and her clothes are clearly off the rack. Did you see her purse?"

"What's wrong with her purse?"

"Nevermind. We'll talk about this when your father gets home, but you know this isn't the plan. You're to marry at or above your social status to retain your trust. I have a list—"

"Fuck the list. I love Penny. End of story." He bolted from his mother and took the stairs two at a time back to Penny's room.

Penny lay on the bed with her sandals off and her hair splayed on the pillow. Seeing her eyes closed, Beckett started to back away, but she reached out to him.

"Sorry, resting my eyes."

He kissed her on the cheek and brushed her hair off her

171

forehead. He loved her so much he thought his heart would burst. "You rest. I'll be back in an hour."

She nodded and closed her eyes.

He escaped out the back door of the mansion and strode down to the basketball court hidden beyond the expansive arborvitae hedge. Beckett had begged for a basketball hoop for his tenth birthday. His mother agreed, as long as it could be hidden from view. He grabbed a ball out of the shed and dribbled it onto the court. He shot basket after basket and chased the rebounds. Sweat poured off his body, and he released his frustrations with his mother. Maybe his father wouldn't be as awful.

* * *

After Penny woke up from her nap, she debated on what to wear for dinner. She stood by the bed in her skivvies trying to decide between her green sundress or blue skirt and blouse.

Beckett knocked and entered her room with damp hair.

"Did you shower?"

"Yeah. I shot some hoops while you rested."

"What should I wear to dinner?"

"This is a brilliant look on you," teased Beckett.

"Stop. Help me."

"I love you in green." Beckett picked the sundress off the bed and handed it to Penny.

"Is it fancy enough?"

"We're eating dinner with my parents, not meeting the queen."

"Are you sure?" she teased.

Penny slipped into the sundress, and Beckett zipped it up and clasped her emerald necklace. She wedged her feet into her low-heeled sandals and held Beckett's hand as he escorted her to the main floor, leading them through halls and around corners. Beckett stopped in front of glass french doors, and they swung open two seconds later. Penny smiled at the girl who opened them, but the girl bent her head and averted her eyes.

They entered the room, stood on the plush white carpet, and faced his parents. His mother had changed out of her suit into a black, silk dress and pulled her hair into a sleek chignon. Beckett's dad wore a gray suit with a pale pink pocket square and matching tie. A butler arrived and asked for their drink orders.

"What would you like to drink?" Beckett asked Penny.

"White wine?"

Beckett asked the butler for wine and a beer before turning his attention to his parents on the couch. "Dad, I'd like you to meet my girlfriend, Penny."

The man stood and clasped both of her hands in his. "Welcome. I hope our accommodations provide you with a respite from your daily life. Beckett tells us you work for an attorney." Penny wasn't sure if his comment was an insult or not, but his clammy hands and acidic breath turned her stomach. When he raked his eyes over her body and settled his leering gaze on her breasts, she yanked her hands from his grasp.

"Yes. I work for an attorney. He handles cases like adoptions and divorces. Family stuff."

Beckett's dad returned to his seat with a sneer. "Small towns and small cases. Must be nice."

Penny had no clue how to respond to the comment, so she pretended to smooth a wrinkle in her dress.

As the staff served them drinks, Beckett led Penny to a couch facing his mother and father. Penny took a seat and sipped her wine. "Your house is beautiful," she said.

Beckett's mother clicked her tongue. "Of course it is."

Beckett coughed and said, "The anniversary party is at

seven tomorrow, right? I'd like to take Penny to the beach during the day."

"Seven, yes. We'll leave at six," said his dad. An awkward silence filled the room. Penny scanned their faces. She couldn't believe they all talked to each other like strangers on a bus instead of family.

A staff member arrived in the doorway. "Dinner is served, ma'am."

They moved into the dining room to a table for twelve. Four place settings of fine china and multiple candelabras graced the long table. Beckett led Penny to one side of the table, and her heart raced when Beckett sat across from her. The expanse of the table was like a wide lake. Geez. They wouldn't even be able to hear each other talk at the huge table.

Her stomach rolled with nausea when she looked down at the place setting. Ten pieces of silverware and three different glasses surrounded her plate, and she didn't know what to do with her current wine glass. She set it to the right of her, and a maid whisked it away. Uniformed men and women arrived in the dining room with the first plate. A man standing by the door announced the food as it entered the room. "Grilled sardines on red pepper coulis with reduced balsamic."

Penny stared at the plate and silverware. Part of the dish was soupy, but there was a fishy thing on top. Beckett picked up a small fork across the table, so she did the same. The red stuff was okay, but she didn't eat the rest. When the plates were cleared, a maid removed her food and replaced the fork. Crap—she must have used the wrong fork. Dinner should never be this stressful.

"Radicchio salad with Stilton, honeyed walnuts, and cabernet," said the man by the door.

A plate was set in front of her—lettuce with cheese and nuts. She chose a different fork and ate a few bites. The pungent cheese coated her tongue—she hid a wince in her napkin. After taking a gulp of water to rid of the taste, she realized no one was talking. How could a family sit around a dinner table and not talk?

"So, what did you do today, Mrs. Young?" she asked.

All eating of the wretched salad stopped, and his parents gaped at her like she'd sprouted horns from her head.

"Yes, Mother. What did you do today?" asked Beckett. He winked at Penny over the table, and she smiled her appreciation in return.

His mother set down her fork and addressed Penny. "I fixed the grocery order and fired the gardener's helper."

Penny assumed someone would pick up the conversation where she left off, but they were interrupted by the third plate of food.

"Wine-braised oxtail with polenta, heirloom carrots, and nasturtium." A flower graced the plate, but she pushed it to the side. She wished Beckett sat beside her so she could whisper to him and ask him questions. The carrots tasted alright, and she tried the meat dish but left the flower. Beckett ate his flower—she hoped he wouldn't get sick later. Dinner progressed with minimal conversation until halfway through their dessert of panna cotta with raspberries.

"The McMillan's daughter returned from her European tour last month and is prepared to be courted, Beckett. You can begin courting her before the holiday parties." Beckett's mother spoke with nonchalance, like she'd said, 'the laundry will be done in an hour.'

Penny inhaled a quick breath, and redness creeped up her neck. If only the ornate chair could swallow her whole.

Beckett slammed his fork down on his plate, and raspberry spattered the tablecloth. "Mother, I love Penny. I won't date another woman."

His mother sipped her tea and set her cup on the saucer. "We'll see."

Penny didn't drink the watery tea in the china cup. She would've given anything for a mug of coffee, but she didn't dare say another word after Beckett's mother had mentioned the arranged courtship with another woman. Desperate to get along with his parents and avoid adding to the tension in the room, she stayed quiet until after dinner when Beckett led her outside to a brick patio the size of a tennis court.

"I'm so sorry," Beckett blurted as soon as they were out of the house. "I can't believe she mentioned the McMillans at the table. You must feel terrible. Let's go to a hotel or go home. Say the word and we're outta here."

A vision of leaving the mansion and checking into one of Beckett's fancy hotel rooms filled her with joy. They could walk the beach and eat a lobster roll as the waves crashed against the shore. Later, they'd play tourists and join a walking tour of historic Boston. It would be so much better than facing his awful parents. However, she pushed the thought aside and said, "No. Family is important. We came here so I could meet your parents. It's only been one meal. It'll get better. Tell me about the McMillan set up."

He ensconced her in his arms. "My mother's agenda won't interfere with us. I'm with you and no one else."

He didn't divulge anything about the McMillans, but she let it go. Penny shuffled on the grass. "Can I ask you a question?"

"Yeah."

"How come you're different from them?"

"They didn't raise me. My parents passed off the day-to-day child rearing to my nanny. Jackson picked up the slack.

Helen wrapped me into her family fold when I was in college. As a kid, it confused me, and it hurt. A lot. Like, when I hit the winning shot in the seventh-grade championship basketball game—they weren't there. Or when I graduated college, they claimed they had a previous engagement. In reality, they refused to sit on the bleachers in a Big Ten stadium." Landscape lights illuminated the obvious pain on his face.

Penny couldn't imagine her parents not attending a college graduation. Her family made the biggest deal about anything. When she got the lead in a musical or received an A on a math test, her parents heaped praise, hugs, and kisses and topped it all off with a trip to the ice cream store. "It's a good thing they didn't raise you."

"I never thought about it like that, but yeah, you're right." They walked around the gardens before retreating inside to Penny's room. They slipped into her bed, where Beckett silenced her questions with kisses. They fused together and made love until the wee hours of the morning.

In the peach bedroom, a sliver of light peeked through the blinds as silky soft sheets slid against Penny's skin. Beckett snored on his back beside her. She rolled over and checked the time on her phone. Six o'clock. Coffee. She needed coffee and a muffin or piece of toast. Her stomach growled from not eating much of the weird meal last night.

She pulled her hair into a loose ponytail, threw on shorts and a Michigan T-shirt, and tiptoed out the door. Beckett rolled to his side but didn't wake up. Her bare feet sank into the plush carpet in the hall and tapped against the marble stairs. A whiff of coffee and bacon hit her nose, and she followed the smells. Quiet voices murmured from a room in the center of the home.

Penny peeked into the room. Beckett's dad, dressed in a suit and tie, sat behind a large desk. His mom, dressed in a cream-colored pantsuit, sat in a leather chair on the other side of the desk. Penny blushed with embarrassment at her shorts and T-shirt. Why were Beckett's parents dressed up at six o'clock in the morning? She was about to go back upstairs and change when she overheard the Youngs talking about her.

"Penny's family is clean," said Beckett's father. "Our private investigator couldn't find a criminal history with any of the O'Briens, but her father is an uneducated electrician in a union—" Beckett's mother gasped. "—The mother is a nurse. The older brothers are mildly successful. Penny has outstanding parking tickets but nothing untoward."

Penny doubled over and gulped air. Beckett's parents investigated her family? Did Beckett know?

"Beckett deserves better. We deserve better."

"He's young. Let him have his fun," said Beckett's dad. "He can't be serious about this girl—he knows the rules. Maybe he could keep Penny as his mistress? It's obvious why he's attracted to her."

"Hmmm," said Beckett's mother. "Not a terrible idea. Have you discussed this option with him?"

"No. I went into his room late last night to talk, but he wasn't there. I peeked into his room on the way down this morning, and his bed was still made. They must have slept together in her room last night. Lucky bastard."

"Don't be crass," said his mother. "They've dated each other since the New Year, I've never seen him so serious."

After a beat of silence, his dad said, "Don't worry. Our plan will work. It'll be over soon."

Penny abandoned the idea of coffee and ran back up the stairs to the peach bedroom. She pressed a hand to her chest to quell the ache. Rules. Mistress. Plan? How could such privileged people be so mean? She climbed back into bed and huddled under the sheets. She wasn't going to be anyone's mistress. Beckett's dad thought their relationship would be over soon. Why? Doubts and reservations filled her mind as she lay in bed beside Beckett. What should she do? Did she love him enough to dismiss the fact his parents had her family investigated? Did he know about it? The bigger question was, could Beckett and Penny's relationship survive the meddling of his parents?

Chapter Twenty-Five

Penny hopped in the shower before Beckett woke up. She didn't want to have a huge discussion about his parents in their house. She planned to attend the party and hash everything out with him on the plane ride home.

Breakfast was similar to the previous nights' dinner, but at least she recognized the food and drank some badly needed coffee. Beckett's father pulled Beckett into his study for an hour. In the meantime, Penny wandered outside. The peonies were in full bloom, and the rose garden belonged on the cover of a magazine. A gardener tended to the flower beds near the tennis courts, and a lawnmower buzzed in the distance. The same question repeated in her mind since she'd eavesdropped on Beckett's parents in the study. How could people this wealthy and privileged be so unkind?

Beckett met her on the lawn after his meeting. He showed her his basketball court and the private pond beyond the rolling hills.

"I would've skated on this pond every day in the winter."

Beckett shook his head. "Let's go to the ocean."

Jackson drove them out the gates of the mansion to the ocean. They strolled the beach before lunch.

Shoes dangled from their fingertips, and the warm wind whipped their faces. They found a place to sit on the beach while little kids jumped in the waves, and families built sandcastles together. Penny dug a hole with her fingers and scooped out the cool sand. "Your parents don't like me."

"They'll come around."

"I'm not so sure."

He stared out to the horizon. "They want me to marry a woman from some list they created years ago. They threaten to dissolve my trust if I marry outside the list. They're bluffing. They'd never do it."

"But we're dating—not getting married," said Penny.

"They want me to marry soon."

A child ran in front of them, flying a kite through the air. "Do you need the trust?" asked Penny.

He threaded his fingers through hers, and the sand scraped her skin. "It's what I'm used to. I like the convenience and the cushion. Money always helped me feel secure."

Penny's family was her security blanket. She could always go home. They never had a lot of things growing up, but they had each other. "What are you going to do if your parents aren't bluffing? What if they take away your trust because you're dating me? Is our love enough for you?"

The questions hung in the air as waves crashed on the shore, and a seagull squawked overhead. There was no way she could compete with a family fortune. It was obvious she didn't fit into his family, but neither one of them wanted to say the words.

· · ·

Penny showered the sand off her body and dressed for the party. A knock sounded on her door as she pinned her hair into a curly updo.

"Beckett?"

"Yeah." He turned the door knob. Beckett whistled low. "Wow."

Penny blushed. "Thanks." Penny stole a glance at Beckett, and a sadness washed over her. She couldn't imagine life without him in it, but reality sank in like a stone tossed into a lake. Beckett would eventually choose her or his family's money. He couldn't have both.

Penny held Beckett's hand as they entered the enormous ballroom. Drinks flowed as small groups gathered around the room. Beckett led Penny to a table they shared with his parents and another couple, along with their two adult children. The other couple air-kissed the Youngs while their son winked at Penny, and their daughter scowled at her.

They took their seats. Penny sipped her water and tried to make sense of the conversation swirling around her. When the topic changed to stock portfolios, Penny rolled her eyes and grabbed her purse. "I'm going to the ladies' room," she whispered to Beckett. Penny's heels clicked on the marble floor as she followed the signs to the restroom. This party was supposed to be fun, but she needed it to be over.

She stood in front of the mirror, touched up her makeup, and fixed her hair. She made small talk with the restroom attendant and checked her email on her phone. Once she was certain she'd wasted enough time, she waved goodbye to the attendant and stepped out into the hallway. On her way back to the ballroom, Beckett's dad rounded a corner and grabbed her elbow—Penny yelped.

"Let's have a chat," he said.

"I need to get back to Beckett." She yanked her arm, but Beckett's dad tightened his grip around her elbow, and his knuckles pressed against the side of her breast.

"He's busy. Let's go in here. I'll get you a drink. White wine, right?" He opened the door to a room with leather chairs and couches. Books lined the shelves along the back wall. Her mind raced. She needed to get away from him, but he guided her to a plush seat and poured white wine and whiskey from a drink cart. He handed her the drink, and her hand shook as she held it on her lap.

Penny scrunched up her nose. "Listen, I need to get back to the table. I'm pretty hungry." She set down her drink and started to stand, but Beckett's dad frowned and barked, "Sit."

Beckett's dad wasn't drunk, but he was tipsy. As she sat back down, he took a seat across from her. He sipped his whiskey and stared at her while he reached into his suit jacket and pulled out a piece of paper.

He handed her the paper, and his face darkened. "You seem like a nice girl. It's unfortunate you come from a...let's say...unremarkable background, but Beckett knows the rules surrounding his trust."

She glanced at the check in her hand. Twenty thousand dollars. Pay to the order of Penny O'Brien.

"Cash it, and never show your face near our family again." He drained his whiskey and left the room.

Penny stared at the check in her shaking hand. Twenty thousand dollars. She'd never seen so much money in one place. Beckett's parents didn't approve of her, but getting rid of her was worth twenty thousand dollars to them? Yikes. Her first instinct was to run back to Beckett and have him defend her, but doubt had wormed its way into her thoughts after their talk on the beach. She didn't know if he loved her more than his money. Part of her didn't want to know the answer. Her phone *dinged* with a text from Beckett.

Are you alright? Where are you?

She stuffed the check into her purse and bolted out of the hotel. Jackson—she needed to find Jackson. With a quick scan of the driveway, she located Jackson talking with other drivers. She ran to him.

"Please drive me back to the house. Now. Please. I don't feel well."

Jackson opened the door, and Penny slid inside the cool, dark car. Her body shook as she sobbed all the way back to the house.

Jackson opened the door for her upon arrival. "Give me five minutes to pack. Can you drive me to the airport?"

"Miss Penny—"

"Please," Penny wailed. She grabbed Jackson's forearm. "I'll be right back." She ran into the house and up the stairs to her room. She whipped off her dress and shoes and threw on jeans and a sweatshirt. She tossed clothes and toiletries into her suitcase before racing down the elegant staircase and handing Jackson her luggage.

Upon their arrival at the airport, Jackson held the door for her and handed her the suitcase. "Miss Penny, I don't know what happened at the party, but you should know, I've never seen Beckett this happy in all his life. He loves you."

"I know." She hugged Jackson, kissed him on the cheek, and ran into the terminal.

Chapter Twenty-Six

BECKETT PUSHED himself away from the table and got up to find Penny. His texts to her went unanswered. He called into the restroom and asked the attendant to search the space. She told him the pretty girl with the red hair and blue dress left the bathroom a while ago. He scanned the hallways and other rooms adjacent to the hotel lobby. When he strode back into the ballroom, regret sliced like a knife through his gut. He never should've brought Penny to Boston.

"Where's Penny?" he asked his parents at the table.

His dad sipped his whiskey, ignoring the question.

Beckett yanked his dad out of his chair, and his drink sloshed over his suit coat. "Where is she?"

"That was easier than I thought it would be," said his dad.

"What did you do?"

"Son, everyone has a price."

Beckett's stomach dropped like a stone. "Penny can't be bought, and neither can I." Beckett turned on his heel and ran out of the ballroom.

· · ·

Jackson was nowhere to be found. An hour and a half later, Beckett tipped his rideshare driver and burst into the mansion. He ran up to the peach room and saw the blue dress strewn across the bed. He gathered the gorgeous gown and held it to his face. Her scent brought tears to his eyes. The rest of her things were gone. He tore off his tux and packed his bag. He paced the foyer until the front door opened—he strode toward his parents.

"Penny's gone."

"Oh, thank goodness," said his mother.

"How much?" Beckett shoved his dad with both of his hands, and he crashed into a family portrait on the wall. The portrait fell and shattered on the floor. His mom shook her head and walked away. Beckett's dad grabbed his wrist before he could shove him again.

"In my study. Now."

"No. Right here. Right now." Beckett yanked his arm away from his dad. Shards of glass skidded around the floor as he jostled his father. "How much?"

"Twenty thousand." His dad smirked. "So easy."

"She'll never cash it."

"We'll see," his dad jeered, "but I wouldn't blame you for keeping her as your mistress—she's got magnificent tits."

Beckett heaved back and threw all his weight into his fist until it collided with his dad's face. His dad bellowed a shout and fell into the shards of glass on the floor. His father's curses echoed in the marble foyer, and a red river of blood flowed down the hall from a cut on his wrist. Beckett stepped over the broken family photo and shook out his hand. He grabbed his luggage and left without another word.

* * *

After two flights and a six-hour layover, Penny arrived home in Misty Lake. A shower washed the grime from the plane off her body, but there was no way to rid herself of the slime from Beckett's parents. She opened her apartment window and let the tears flow.

Chapter Twenty-Seven

During summer in the Boundary Waters, Misty Lake bustled with tourists and busy friends. Emma taught classes at Mark's Gere, Beth worked long hours at the café, and Kelly pulled double shifts at Northern Woods. Beckett called and texted Penny every day, but she deleted his text messages, dismissed his calls, and ignored his voicemails. She didn't want to be embroiled in his family shenanigans, but she missed him so much. There were days she thought her heart had cracked in half.

Penny stumbled late into work again.

"Penny, you need some time off," said Drew.

"I'm fine." She turned on her desk lamp and picked up the envelope lying on her computer.

Drew shuffled from foot to foot. "Um, I wasn't sure how to tell you, but Beckett's gala for *Ripple Effects* is coming up. You can ride to Minneapolis with me and Kelly if you want."

The seats were a hundred dollars each. A part of her wanted to go celebrate and support his success. He'd worked so hard to honor Helen's last wish. Even so, she knew seeing him would destroy her. "I'll think about it."

Penny's leaden body sweat in the summer heat of her studio apartment. One day, in early July, she rented a solo canoe from Northern Woods and pushed it into the lake. The hot, sunny day kept anglers off the water.

She paddled around until a loon wailed long and loud. Another loon joined in the chorus. The lonesome sound penetrated her soul, and she paddled to shore. She collapsed on the bench and cried with them.

After the canoe ride, she gave up on trying to heal by herself and drove home to her parents' house.

Tears spilled down Penny's cheeks when her mother opened her arms for her. They sat on the back patio with lemonade and cookies. Her mom listened as Penny described the wretched weekend in Boston, the bribe, and how she loved Beckett, but their relationship was doomed.

"Beckett and I would never work. He's got this trust, and it tethers him to his family. If we ever got really serious, Beckett would have to choose between me and the money." Penny ate another cookie and slouched in the patio chair. She tilted her head back and closed her eyes against the tears as the sun beat down on her face.

"What did you do with the money?" asked her mom.

Penny sat up and gasped. The check. Where was it? She couldn't remember what she did with it. "It must still be in my purse." She grabbed her purse off the ground beside her and scrounged around inside. She pulled the crumpled check from the bottom of the bag—the sight of it made her recoil.

Her mom leaned over her shoulder. "Twenty thousand

dollars is a lot of money to be carrying around in the bottom of your purse."

Penny couldn't believe it. "I was so upset about Beckett, I totally forgot about the actual check."

"Are you going to cash it?"

She stared at the check. "I'm going to donate it."

"Good for you."

Penny slipped the check back into her purse. They sat silent and let the birds be the only noise in the backyard.

"My parents didn't approve of your dad at the beginning," said her mom.

Penny raised her head and opened her eyes. "They didn't? They love him now."

Her mom poured more lemonade into their glasses before taking a long drink. "I was in college getting my nursing degree. My friends and I went to a fraternity party the first weekend of sophomore year. The party spilled onto the lawn, and my girl-friends and I danced in the front yard. This guy I didn't recognize caught my eye. I'll never forget his half smile and small wave as he leaned against the fence. I waved back to him and... he asked me to dance.

"The full moon and warm, humid air were the perfect recipe for romance. We swayed to the music until cop cars surrounded the house, and people dumped drinks and scat-tered. There was a lot of yelling, and I couldn't find my girl-friends anywhere, but the guy took my hand, and we hopped a hedge in the backyard and ran for three blocks. We slowed to a walk near a city park, and the first thing he asked me was, 'Are you alright?' He didn't ask me my name or what my major was, he asked if I was alright."

Penny froze in her seat. Those were the exact same first words Beckett said to her when they collided before Helen's funeral. More tears pooled in her eyes. "Classic Dad. Always making sure everyone is safe and healthy."

"My whole body tingled," her mom continued. "There was this...energy between us. We dated for a month before he told me he loved me. But your father wasn't a student at the university. He was a townie—an apprentice electrician in town, and he loved his job. He crashed the fraternity party with some of his friends but never had any plans for a college education. He was well-read and well-mannered, but my parents demanded I break up with him and find a 'nice college boy.'"

Her mom sipped some lemonade. "Three months later, we married and lived in married-student housing on campus. We worked together to pay for the rest of my college education because your grandfather stopped paying when I married your dad."

"Oh, Mom. I had no idea. That must have been really tough. Did they come to your wedding?"

"They did, but you've seen the pictures. Your grandmother looks like she's being dragged off into the woods by bears. Your grandfather refused to give a speech at the reception and made an excuse to skip his dance with me."

Penny's heart clenched as her mom shared her pain. "My parents didn't accept us until your brother came along. Grandchildren have a way of bringing families together." Penny's mom folded her hands in her lap. "I'll tell you the most important thing I remember about that time in my life. I knew, deep down in my soul, your dad and I belonged together. And nothing, not even my parents' disapproval, was going to stop me from being with him."

* * *

In the second week of July, Beckett wore his earbuds for his commercial flight to Boston, where he was squished between a large man and a young woman with a baby. He closed his eyes and envisioned Penny.

He rented an economy-sized car and drove home. Instead of going inside to greet his parents like usual, he drove around the back to the service wing of the mansion. When he walked through the door, he found Jackson playing cards with another driver.

Jackson jumped up from his chair. "Mister Beckett. Your travel wasn't on the schedule. I would've picked you up at the airport."

Beckett flung himself at Jackson and collapsed into his arms for a fierce hug. "Can I pull you away from your game? I have news."

"Let's walk," said Jackson.

They went outside, and Beckett shoved his hands in his pockets. His hair blew from the warm breeze off the ocean. "First, thank you for taking care of Penny on the night of the anniversary party."

Jackson nodded.

"I came home to talk with my parents." As usual, Jackson let him talk and didn't interrupt. "I've given up my trust and separated from my parents financially. I love Penny, and I don't want money to be a factor in our relationship. I earn a decent living. I won't be using the car service anymore, and I got rid of the plane last week. Mother and Father won't want me around, but I want to stay in touch with you. I...love you and want you to know you'll always be in my life."

Jackson stopped and removed his hat. "This is a job, but you and I—we'll always be family."

Beckett wiped away a tear. They walked through the small

orchard behind the pool and talked until he skewered up the courage to go inside the home.

His mother and father sat across from each other on love seats in one of the sitting rooms near the ballroom. When Beckett walked through the door, his father set down his phone, and his mother sipped her bourbon. It was the first time he'd seen them since the night of the anniversary party.

"Hello, dear," said his mother. "You mentioned in your message that you had something to discuss with us. I have to get to the club soon and your father is playing a round of golf at four. Will this take long?"

Beckett shook his head. "Nope. I came to tell you I've applied for a qualified disclaimer and released the trust. I love Penny, and I choose her."

His father smirked.

"But...my plan," said his mother. "What will everyone say?"

Beckett turned to his mother. "Not my problem. I never agreed to the plan. I was just unfortunate enough to be born into it."

"She cashed the check," said his father. "You owe me twenty grand if she ever speaks to you again."

Beckett recoiled like he'd been hit in the gut with a baseball bat, but he tried not to let the hurt show on his face. He narrowed his eyes toward his father. "I don't believe you."

His father tossed the rest of his whiskey down his throat and pulled his phone off the table. He scrolled several times before holding it up to Beckett's face—a copy of the deposited check appeared on his phone with Penny's signature.

Beckett shook his head, desperate to wipe away the visual of the cashed check. He took a breath to compose himself. "Spend your money however you want, but I've got a pretty cool charity in need of some cash. Let me know if you'd like to donate." Beckett left a business card for *Ripple Effects* on the coffee table. He walked out a side door of the mansion and drove the rental car down the winding road and past the gates.

Once out of sight, he pulled the car over and shoved the gear shift into park. He pounded the dash. His breath caught in his throat. "No, no, no." He didn't want to believe his father. Penny would never accept a bribe. Would she? The picture of the cashed check seared into his brain. Maybe he didn't know her as well as he thought he did.

The used Jeep bounced on the road as Beckett drove to the Cincinnati suburbs with his arm out the window. He didn't want any reminders of the trust, so he'd hired a realtor to find a new home. He slowed as he entered the neighborhood and smiled at children riding bikes and families grilling dinner in the backyard. A little girl played hopscotch in her driveway, and two teens shot baskets in a cul-de-sac.

He turned down a tree-lined street and parked in front of a white colonial with black shutters. One of the gutters sagged in the front, and the sidelight had a crack, but he loved the white picket fence, the wide front porch, and the basketball hoop hanging on the garage door.

"Ready to see another, Mr. Young?" asked his realtor.

"Yep. I'm excited about this one. It looks like it may need some work, but it's in my price range."

His realtor led him through the home built in the eighties. The kitchen needed new cabinets and counters, and the carpet in the bedrooms had worn thin. The primary bedroom had an ensuite bathroom with a chipped sink, and some of the wall colors were crazy. But when they went out the back door to the brick patio, he knew he found his house. A tire swing hung from a large oak tree in the backyard like he dreamed of as a kid.

"What do you think?" asked his realtor.

"It needs work, and I can't wait to get started. Let's put in an offer."

His repeated calls to Penny went straight to voicemail. Didn't she ever listen to his messages? He left countless voicemails apologizing for his parents and telling her he broke away from them financially. One sappy call reiterated his boundless love for her. Another call detailed the return of the plane and the sale of his Jaguar. After his voicemail telling her he'd moved out of the condo and into the suburbs, he stopped calling her. He needed to see her in person. He'd go to Misty Lake immediately after the gala. She couldn't turn him down in person, right? He returned his focus to *Ripple Effects*—there were a million details that needed his attention.

Chapter Twenty-Eight

In July, a community theater in Duluth posted auditions for the musical *Grease*. Penny signed up for the audition and prepped the music and dancing over the next couple of weeks. Drew awarded her with time off to rehearse at the church and travel to the audition. When she stepped onto the stage, adrenaline surged. She rocked the audition, but she didn't want to get her hopes up.

A call back was posted the next day, and Penny drove to the theater for a second time. The director was kind and helpful, and Penny nailed the choreography once again. When the final cast list was posted, her name was next to the starring role of Sandy. Relief flooded her, and she drove back to Misty Lake with new confidence.

In August, Penny's time was consumed by rehearsals for *Grease*. She worked early morning hours for Drew and drove to rehearsals in the afternoon. The small community theater didn't pay anything, but the experience could propel her to bigger roles. Her crazy schedule also meant the pain of missing Beckett didn't hurt until her head hit the pillow.

. . .

The night of the *Ripple Effects* gala, she rode to Minneapolis
with Drew and Kelly. Mark and Emma drove separately. Kelly
talked non-stop in the car, and Penny murmured the occasional
'mhmm' and 'uh-huh' but couldn't focus on anything besides
what to say to Beckett. She hadn't listened to any of his voicemails or returned his calls. It was for the best. Besides, tonight
was for Helen—at least that's what she told herself. She picked
her thumbnail and hummed her *Grease* pieces to take her mind
off the event.

Drew dropped them off at the door, and Penny peeked in
the ballroom at the beautiful tables. Beckett's elegant touch was
all over them, and all of the ideas they'd talked about were
there: the table names on miniature canoe paddles, fairy lights
inside a trio of candle votives for the centerpieces, pictures of
kids on canoe trips flashing on the side walls of the ballroom,
and a chocolate loon on the plate of every place setting.

Their group found their table. Everyone engaged in conversation with each other, but Penny's stomach roiled—she
couldn't stop looking for Beckett. When he emerged from a
side door in a black suit to greet each group of guests, she
rubbed the tight knot in her chest. Her body heated, and her
muscles tensed as he approached their table. How did she ever
survive the last few months? She wanted to forget all about his
slimy parents and leap into his arms. She wanted to tell him all
about her role in *Grease* and how proud she was of him for
creating the nonprofit. She cleared her throat and sipped her
water. Though hesitant, she gave him a small wave, and Beckett's gorgeous blue eyes went wide. Penny couldn't pull her
gaze from him even when he turned away from her to welcome
their friends.

"Thanks for coming, everyone. I appreciate your support

for a great cause. Enjoy the appetizers, and dinner will begin soon. I'm waiting for the band to arrive." He waved and began moving on to another group.

Penny grabbed the envelope with the twenty-thousand-dollar check for *Ripple Effects* from her purse. She got up and caught his arm before he reached the next table. "Can we talk for a minute?"

He snatched his elbow away and whirled around. "Now?" he said in a harsh whisper. "You want to talk now? I've called you a hundred times since you ditched me in Boston. I'm in the middle of the event. I need to go." Beckett spun on his heel and went to the next table.

Penny touched her cheek as if she'd been slapped. She made a dash for the lobby and ran to the bathroom. Why was he mad at her? Because she didn't answer a few calls? His father investigated her family and tried to bribe her with twenty thousand dollars; she was the one who should be mad. Whatever. Drew would make sure the check was deposited into the charity. She splashed some water on her face and found her way back to the table.

The stuffed mushrooms and bruschetta tasted like sawdust, and the steak and shrimp dinner didn't have any flavor. She pushed the food around on her plate, but the rest of the guests raved about the meal. Even Kelly gave the caterers high praise. Silverware clinked, and the steady hum of conversation filled the space, but there wasn't any music. Where was the band Beckett's board hired instead of her?

Before dessert, Penny excused herself to freshen her makeup. She noticed Drew and Beckett in a heated discussion at the end of the hall. Beckett's face paled—he was frantic. She turned around, not wanting to face the wrath of Beckett again, but Drew called her name.

"Penny?"

"Yeah?"

"We have a problem. The band got in a car accident on the way to the event and aren't coming. We can't find a DJ. The gala invitation promised dinner and dancing."

Penny looked from Drew to Beckett. She shoved her hurt and anger aside and turned to Beckett. "I've got this. Let me check my makeup, and I'll meet you backstage in ten minutes."

The surprised look on Beckett's face was replaced with relief. "Thank you so much."

Beckett paced the wood floor beside a grand piano when Penny arrived backstage. "You've saved my ass. Thanks."

"No problem."

They stared at each other for a long moment. She couldn't deny her love for him despite what happened in Boston. They needed to talk. About everything. She should've answered his calls...Was it too late?

Beckett left to introduce her to the crowd. Penny played and sang song after song for the donors who danced late into the night.

Chapter Twenty-Nine

During the drive from Duluth to Misty Lake, Penny listened to pop tunes on the car's radio and drummed her fingers to the beat on the steering wheel. *Grease* rehearsals lengthened the two weeks before opening night, but the cast worked hard, and Penny loved everything about the experience. Between work and rehearsals, the pain of missing Beckett dulled but resurfaced at odd times. Little things reminded her of him, like kids playing basketball in the park, a smooth voice over the radio, or dimples on strangers.

One night after rehearsal, the costume designer needed to check Penny's measurements, causing her to leave the auditorium later than usual. She was ten miles outside of Duluth when her car sputtered, and the check engine light flashed on the dashboard. After another mile, smoke poured out of her hood—she couldn't see the road. Penny pulled over to the shoulder and stopped. She went out to investigate why her car had overheated, and she popped open the hood. Smoke billowed and hissed from the old car, and staring at the stuff inside of it wasn't helping the problem. Penny didn't have much choice but to call a tow truck.

A dispatcher told her it would be an hour before anyone arrived. Penny sighed but thanked the woman and hung up. She should've taken her car to be serviced months ago. Ugh. She leaned against her car on the dark autumn night and left a voicemail for Drew.

"Hey, I might be late to work tomorrow morning. My car overheated on the way home from rehearsal tonight, and I called a tow. See ya."

Lights swooped around the bend. This wasn't the tow truck already, was it? Rust ran along the side of the gray truck, and the rearview mirror hung askew. Dents covered the front, and the tailgate wasn't square. The truck slowed, and a teenager with a wild look on his face called out his window.

"Get in."

"Oh, no, thanks. I called a tow truck. My car started smoking and got really hot, ya know? They'll be along soon."

The driver parked and bolted from his truck. He crossed the road and approached her. "Get in." He growled and shoved her toward the truck, and her phone flew out of her hand.

"Hey! Cut it out," Penny said as she wrenched her arm from the teen. When she reached down to grab her phone, he kicked it away and pushed her into the driver side of the pickup truck. A teen girl sat in the passenger seat and cradled her swollen belly with a grimace on her face. The boy got back behind the wheel and gunned the engine. Wedged in between the pregnant girl and, presumably, her boyfriend, Penny turned around to see her car disappear out the window.

"We need your help," said the boy.

"Oh. Well . . ."

"My girlfriend's in pain. Real bad."

They flew down the road, and every time the guy turned a corner, the pregnant girl clutched her belly. "I'm not a doctor or a nurse. I work for an attorney and sing, too." Penny couldn't seem to stop talking. "My dream is to sing and dance on Broadway. I don't think I can help your girlfriend. Why don't we call a doctor?"

Neither teen answered her, and she cursed herself for not taking better care of her car. They drove for two or three miles on the highway back toward Duluth and turned down a gravel road. They bumped around in the truck through woods, blackness engulfing them.

The vehicle slowed to a stop in front of a tent in a clearing. The guy and the girl shuffled out of the truck and into the tent.

The guy stuck his head out of the tent. "Come on. You need to help."

Penny jumped from the truck and lifted the tent flap with her hand. "What are you doing? You should be at a hospital. Come on, I'll go with you. Let's get back in the truck."

The girl spoke for the first time. "No," she sniffled. "We planned to have the baby here. A friend of mine was supposed to help, but she chickened out. Please help me."

Penny sat on the ground beside the girl and held her hand. "My name is Penny. What's yours?"

"Cassie."

"Okay, Cassie. Here's the deal. I'm not a nurse or a doctor. I don't know anything about having babies or delivering babies, but I'll do my best to help you." Cassie gripped her hand, and a wave of pain crossed her face. She wailed during the contraction and whimpered when it left her body. Penny said, "Cassie, I'll be right back."

She motioned for the guy hovering on the other side of Cassie to follow her outside.

Once outside, she put her hands on her hips and spoke in a controlled whisper. "What the fuck? You drag me off the side of the road and into your truck to bring me to a tent to help your girlfriend give birth? She needs medical help. I know nothing about this, but I'm guessing this isn't the safest place for her to have a baby. Why are you out here, and why didn't you take her to a hospital?"

The tough guy from the truck suddenly resembled a kid barely out of middle school. His pale face gave away his fright. "Her parents hate me. I have a stupid dad who doesn't care about me, but Cassie's parents are, like, all involved in her life. We love each other, but they *despise* me. We hid the baby from everyone until a few weeks ago. Her mom found out and told her we couldn't see each other anymore. Cassie snuck out of the house when she went into labor."

"What's your name?"

"Dennis."

"How old are you?"

He straightened his shoulders. "Gonna be eighteen real soon."

"And Cassie?"

"Almost seventeen."

Penny shuddered. Sixteen-year-olds should be sharing fries and sodas with girlfriends after school or holding hands with a love interest in the movie theater. Sixteen was for football games and homecoming and learning how to drive—not becoming a mother.

"I thought when she started wailing, the baby was gonna be here fast."

"I don't know much, but I know first babies take longer. When did the pain start?"

The guy squinted his eyes and thought. "Maybe two hours ago?"

"We have time. Let's go."

Chapter Thirty

THE BUZZING BEE PERSISTED, and Beckett slapped the air to make it stop. Again, it buzzed. Beckett slapped his pillow, but the faint buzz sounded again, waking him. Still dark, he reached a hand out from under the covers to the phone masquerading as a bee on the nightstand. He tapped the screen without looking and mumbled, "Hello."

"Sorry to wake you, but I thought you'd want to know," said Drew.

"Know what?"

"Penny's missing."

Beckett bolted up in bed and glanced at the clock. Two in the morning. "What?"

"The cops called me. They found her phone on the side of the highway between here and Duluth. Her car broke down on the way back from a rehearsal. She called a tow, but when the truck showed up, Penny wasn't there. Her purse was in the car, and her phone was found on the road, but she was missing. The tow truck guy called the cops. When the detective managed to get into her phone, they discovered her last phone call was to me. She left a message for me last night about being late to work in the morning. The cops called me, and I'm on my way to the Duluth police station."

Beckett broke out in a cold sweat. He'd leapt out of bed before Drew finished the story. He couldn't imagine a world where Penny was gone. Even if she did cash his dad's bribe, he still loved her. "On my way."

* * *

"AAGH," Cassie yelled as she got into the truck. Penny hummed a folk tune in her ear, hoping to help Cassie work through the pain. The truck sputtered a few times, but the engine turned over, and Dennis sped down the road. Cassie clenched in pain before they reached a rural hospital on the outskirts of town. Dennis and Penny helped Cassie into the facility, and Penny explained to the receptionist that Cassie was in labor. A nurse loaded Cassie into a wheelchair and told both Penny and Dennis to sit in the orange plastic chairs.

Penny studied her abductor—a frightened young man who *should* be playing video games with his buddy on a Thursday night, not kidnapping some stranger off a highway to help his pregnant girlfriend. "Um, when the nurse comes back, I'm going to use her phone to call my boss and explain why I won't be at work today."

Dennis hung his head. "I'm sorry. I'm not usually an asshole. Honest."

"Good to know. How 'bout you call Cassie's mom? I'm sure they're really worried."

He shook his head. "Nah. I can't. They hate me."

"Call them, and tell them their grandchild is about to be born."

The teenager got up from the orange chair and scrolled his phone on the other side of the room.

The nurse reappeared. "Penny, Cassie is asking for you."

"Oh, but I need to—"

"Now."

Penny scowled and hustled through the double doors. She could hear Cassie before the nurse pulled back the curtain. Penny went to Cassie's side and held her hand.

"Sing. The singing helps me with the pai . . ." Cassie grimaced as another contraction wracked her body. Penny sang.

* * *

Beckett bought a flight going from Cincinnati to Duluth with a layover in Minneapolis. It was set to depart at five in the morning—he would need to rush. When he reached the airport, the parking garage was full. He navigated back to long-term parking and waited for the shuttle to the terminal. At security, the guy in front of him argued with an agent about how he should be able to take his full bottle of water to his gate. When Beckett was finally through security, he tied his shoes with the rest of humanity and growled at commercial air travel. He would've already been in the air with his private jet.

Even though his calls to Penny's phone went unanswered, he filled her voicemail with messages while he waited at the gate. When he touched down in Duluth, it was late morning, and the line at the car-rental kiosk was twenty deep. How did people travel like this all the time?

Beckett bolted through the door of the police station and found Drew talking with a cop. He shook Drew's hand before introducing himself to the detective.

"What do we know? How can I help?"

The detective glanced up from his computer and raised an eyebrow at Beckett. "We've got officers searching the area surrounding the scene. Ms. O'Brien probably walked to a home nearby for food or a bathroom. There weren't any signs of force or trauma at the scene. Her discarded phone gives us pause, but it's only been a few hours."

The words 'scene,' 'trauma,' and 'signs of force' sent a chill through Beckett's body like he was stranded naked on a glacier at the North Pole. "What can we do?" he asked the detective.

"Wait. Let us do our jobs."

* * *

At seven o'clock in the morning, a doctor examined Cassie and pronounced she was ready to push. Penny squeezed Cassie's hand and pushed with her. An hour later, Cassie's wails were replaced with the high-pitched cry of a newborn baby. Dennis joined them in the room, and the young teens basked in the glow of love and awe for their newborn. He cradled the baby and kissed Cassie on the forehead. She gazed up at him like he had every answer in the whole world. Penny stepped back from the private moment and asked to use a phone at the nurses' station. Drew's work phone rang and rang, so she tried his cell.

"Drew?"

"Penny?!" screamed Drew into the phone. "Where are you?"

Before she could answer, Beckett's silky voice came over the line sounding more jagged than she'd ever heard him. "Are you hurt? Where are you?"

"Beckett? Drew? Yes. Yes. I'm okay. I've had quite a night, but I'm fine. I'm at a small hospital outside of Duluth."

"Are you hurt?" Beckett's ragged voice broke as he spoke.

"No. I'm not hurt. I'm fine, but I've lost my phone, and I don't know what happened to my car."

Drew's voice came back on the line. "The Duluth police have your phone, and your car is fixed and waiting for you at an auto shop here."

"Where are you guys?"

"The Duluth police station," said Beckett. "The detective needs to talk to you."

Penny spoke with the detective, and he told her an officer would bring her to the police station. She sat in an orange plastic chair, waiting for her ride, when the hospital doors burst open, and a middle-aged couple ran to the reception desk. Presuming they were Cassie's parents, Penny said a little prayer for the new family and hoped her mother's wisdom held true— she hoped the new grandchild would bring the families together.

Upon her arrival at the Duluth police station, Penny found three things: her phone, her boss, and a frantic Beckett. She sat with the detective, and everyone listened to her story. Penny didn't press charges against Dennis. The teen parents deserved a clean start to their new life together. Someone brought her a sandwich in the middle of all the paperwork, and the trio left the station in the late afternoon.

They stood on the sidewalk in the fading light. Beckett told Drew to head back to Misty Lake and said that he'd drive Penny to her car. Penny hugged Drew and told him they'd catch up tomorrow. She slid into the passenger seat of Beckett's rental car and sighed, closing her eyes. Ten minutes later, Beckett put the car in park, and Penny opened her eyes. They were outside the auto shop. Parked in the space beside them was her old and battered but well-loved vehicle. "Why didn't you buy a car with the money?" asked Beckett.

Penny stared into Beckett's clear blue eyes. She was speechless for a moment…"You thought I kept the money?"

"You endorsed and cashed the check."

"The check is cashed, but I didn't keep the money." Tired, irritated, and hurt, Penny unbuckled her seat belt and opened the door. She turned back to Beckett. "I thought we knew each other."

* * *

Penny's question haunted him. *You thought I kept the money?* It sounded ridiculous now. She wouldn't cash a twenty-thousand-dollar bribe. She had trouble accepting help up a flight of icy stairs.

If she hadn't kept the money, though, what *did* she do with it?

Chapter Thirty-One

Labor Day dawned, cool but sunny, and Penny drove through town to join the festivities at Mark and Emma's house. Exhausted from working full-time and traveling to rehearsals for the show, she sat in a folding chair on Mark and Emma's lawn. Drew and Kelly teased each other over a corn hole game, and families canoed on the lake or played volleyball. Beth flirted with the local pharmacist near the lake, and Emma sauntered over with a hot dog for her.

Penny accepted it with a smile. "Thanks. I was just about to go to the grill and snag a dog. Do you have time to sit for a minute?"

"Sure." Emma plopped into Kelly's empty chair beside her and sighed. "How are you?"

"Rehearsals are going well, and I'm trying to keep up with the job, but I need to talk to Drew about reducing my hours to part-time."

"No. *How are you?*"

Penny shrugged. "Okay, I guess. A year ago, I was laser

focused on my dream and earning money to become independent. I have that, but now . . ."

"Beckett?"

Penny's eyes filled with tears, and she nodded. "I miss him so much. We need to talk, but I've been so busy with work and the musical, and I've booked gigs in Nashville and Pittsburgh right after the show."

Emma squeezed her arm. "Have you listened to his messages?"

Penny shook her head.

"Make the time, and listen to them."

Penny ate another bite of her hot dog, and Emma clutched her stomach and breathed deep. "Emma? You alright?"

Emma blushed. "I'm fine. A little nausea."

Penny shifted back in her chair and blanched. "My show is next week—I can't get sick."

Emma laughed and winked at her. "My pregnancy won't make you sick."

Penny gasped. "Ooh! I'm so excited for you." She wrapped an arm around her friend. "You're gonna be such a good momma."

After two more hours of pretending to enjoy herself, Penny retreated to the parking lot and got into her car. Emma was right, she needed to listen to Beckett's voicemails. She drove toward Northern Woods for peace and quiet. The Labor Day guests were either tromping through the woods or on the lake because the property was deserted. Penny walked down the hill and sat on the bench beside the lake. She could almost hear the pain in Beckett's voice on the day of Helen's funeral and his laughter when he skated on the lake for the first time.

She pulled her phone out of her purse and scanned the messages. She scrolled back to the first voicemail from Beckett after she'd left Boston and hit play. Tears pierced her eyes from the sound of his voice. Voicemail after voicemail filled in the details from the moment he left his parents' house the night of the anniversary party. Penny's head spun like a merry go round as she listened.

He explained his financial break from his parents, the sale of the Jaguar, how he got rid of the plane, and the purchase of his new house. He told her that he wanted to talk, he missed her, and he loved her. Every voicemail ended with an 'I love you' and a plea to call him.

Barring the voicemail from the night she'd helped the teens deliver their baby, Beckett's last voicemail was from weeks ago. He must have given up on her.

A breeze blew from the lake, and Penny wiped her wet face. Beckett deserved more than a phone call. She needed to go see him.

Chapter Thirty-Two

OPENING night always gave her the jitters, and tonight was no different. She warmed up with the cast of *Grease* and sat for the makeup artist. Understudies prowled around backstage, waiting for their chance, but Penny's confidence didn't waiver. Her entire family would be in the audience, and all her friends from Misty Lake procured opening night tickets to the show in Duluth. Drew secured a private room in a restaurant for an after party, and she couldn't wait to celebrate with everyone.

Roaring applause and three curtain calls followed the show. Her friends and family were all in the front row, standing on their feet at the end of the production. She took her bows and blew a kiss to the audience. A tall man with brown, wavy hair caught her eye as he exited the back row. Beckett? She squinted into the dark theater, but she couldn't see a thing with the house lights off. Before she could give Beckett another thought, the cast pulled her off stage left, and the curtain came down.

When she finally reached her dressing room, a large bouquet of pale pink roses waited for her. The card read: *Congratulations, Penny. You were phenomenal. I'm so proud of you. —A lonely loon.* She clutched the card from Beckett and inhaled the sandalwood and vanilla scent. He must have had the card in his jacket or suit pocket. She ran into the lobby and scoured every corner, but Beckett was nowhere to be found. Maybe he'd be at the afterparty.

She hurried out of her outfit and scrubbed as much of the makeup off her face as she could before yanking on her jeans and a sweater. She gathered her purse, drove to the restaurant Drew reserved, and hustled inside.

Her family and friends cheered as she entered the room, and she accepted hugs and kisses from everyone. Once her brothers stopped teasing her, she pulled Drew aside and said, "Where's Beckett? He left me flowers in my dressing room. I thought he'd be here."

Drew's smile faded. "I told him about the show, but I didn't invite him to the after party because I didn't want to freak you out and ask ahead of time. I thought it might screw up your performance. I'm sorry. Should I have asked him?"

Penny hid her disappointment and said, "No, no. You're right. I would've freaked for sure. Good call. I just wanted to thank him for the flowers."

Drew held her arm and stared at her. "Call him."

* * *

The week after Penny's opening night, Beckett met with his board of directors and Drew in their office space in Minneapolis for *Ripple Effects'* monthly meeting. The main topic of discussion was the successful gala fundraiser. The event planner touted the success of the venue and food and praised Drew and Beckett's recovery of the entertainment portion of the evening. The treasurer announced the funds raised and, in particular, pointed out one generous, anonymous donor.

"Well, not anonymous, but we don't have a name. The donor was . . ." the woman consulted her spreadsheet on her laptop, "here it is—'Lonely Loon.'"

Beckett's head snapped up, and he searched Drew's face. Drew winked at him and smiled. "What did you say?" he asked the treasurer.

"The donor signed the paperwork 'Lonely Loon.'"

"How much was the check for?"

"Twenty thousand."

Penny. It had to be Penny. She did cash the check—for Helen. Love swelled in his chest, and he nearly levitated off the chair. He couldn't wait to be done with the meeting.

Beckett shoved his laptop and papers into his briefcase and cornered Drew after the meeting. "'Lonely Loon' is Penny, right?"

"She brought the check to the gala, but you argued, and then she bailed you out with her performance. She didn't want to mess with it during the event and gave it to me the next day. She asked me to deposit it with the name 'Lonely Loon.' I wasn't sure what she meant, but I followed through."

Beckett's heart slammed against his chest. "I need to see her. Now. Tonight. Can I ride back to Misty Lake with you? I took a rideshare from the airport today."

"You can ride back with me to Misty Lake, but Penny's not there. She's got gigs in Nashville and Pittsburgh the next two weeks."

His shoulders slumped.

"She'll be back in Misty Lake in a few weeks."

Beckett wasn't sure he could wait that long.

Chapter Thirty-Three

The wedding in Nashville didn't disappoint. The traditional church ceremony was followed by the drunk groom groping a server and the bride tossing a glass of wine in his face. Penny pocketed her check and hustled out of the venue.

The drive to Cincinnati the next day was a short four hours, and she arrived earlier than anticipated. A mixture of fear and trepidation filled her as she checked into the downtown hotel and dumped her stuff in the room. The plan was to surprise Beckett at his house in the suburbs tomorrow and have the conversation they should've had months ago. Restless and nervous, Penny went back outside for a stroll along the riverwalk to stretch her legs.

In the park adjacent to the riverwalk, the thumps of basketballs caught her attention. She squinted her eyes toward the noise. She couldn't remember if this was the exact park where Beckett played with his buddies, but it could be. She picked up her pace and crossed into the park. As she got closer, she found six men running around the court. Wavy hair bounced in the air. It was him. He was here. His arms flexed when he passed the ball. Oh, how she wanted those arms around her again. She picked up her pace and was about to shout his name when a woman from the other side of the park approached the side lines. Penny halted and watched.

Beckett called time out and jogged over to the woman. He hugged her. They had a short, laughter-filled conversation and exchanged smiles. Then, he kissed her on the cheek and hugged her again. Penny gasped, her face heating. He had a girl. He had a girl. She kept repeating it over and over again in her head. She had to get out of there. Beckett couldn't see her now.

She flipped her collar up on her coat and went back toward her hotel from the backside of the park. When she was out of view, she found a bench on the riverwalk and held her head in her hands. She was so stupid. It never crossed her mind. Of course Beckett had a new woman in his life. He was a catch. Handsome, smart, kind, and lovable. She couldn't show up unannounced at his house now. What if the woman lived with him? Tears dripped onto the pavement and formed wet circles on the asphalt.

"Are you alright, dear?" A woman with white hair sat beside her and offered her a tissue.

Penny wiped her face with the back of her hand and shook her head. "Normally, I'd tell you I was fine. Because I'm always fine. But I'm not fine. I pushed the love of my life away, and now he's with another woman."

The woman patted her arm. "Oh, my. You must have had a good reason to end things?"

Penny sniffled. "Yeah."

"You loved him, though."

"More than coffee or loons or singing."

"Have faith, my dear. A true love story never ends."

Penny blew her nose in the tissue, and the old woman hobbled away.

The sun set on the walk back to the hotel. If she packed now, she'd be able to make it halfway to Pittsburgh tonight. She dressed in comfortable clothes to drive and packed her suitcase. The hotel clerk charged her for the early checkout, but she didn't care or fight the charge. She needed to get out of Cincinnati.

In the underground garage, she started her car without a problem and plugged in directions to Pittsburgh. Tears blurred her vision as she pulled into rush hour traffic. Horns honked, and a man gave her the finger when she ran a yellow light. She hissed a swear word, missed an exit, and had to go around another city block. Her phone rang, and she bent down to answer Emma's call. By the time she raised her head, she'd swerved to the right and slammed into the bumper of a Jeep.

"Shit, shit, shit." She pulled over to the side of the road behind the Jeep and got out.

"Penny?" Beckett stood beside the Jeep. "Are you alright?"

Penny swiveled from the Jeep, to Beckett, to her car, and back again. "This is your car?"

"Yeah. You dented me this time." He rubbed the dent. "And I don't have a lot of money for repairs this month." Beckett dragged a hand through his hair and held her gaze.

"What?" Cars whizzed by—Penny strained to hear him. She peered over his shoulder to see if the girl from the park was in the car.

"What are you doing here?" Beckett yelled over the traffic.

Penny moved closer to him so he could hear her. "I was at the park an hour ago. You hugged a girl."

"You were at the park?"

"Yeah. I came to see you. I mean, I wanted to see you. I miss you." Penny's words were swallowed by a semi-truck passing them on the road. "Who's the girl?"

"What girl?"

She yelled into his ear, "You hugged a girl at the park."

"My best friend's fiancée?" he yelled back to her. "I helped her with a birthday gift for him."

"Oh."

An ambulance siren screamed on the road. "I can't hear you," he shouted. "Listen, come to my house. I'll text you the address." Beckett hopped back into his Jeep and pulled into traffic.

Beckett's neighborhood was full of leaf piles and pumpkins on porches, and his house sat at the bottom of a cul-de-sac. She parked her car behind his mailbox. When she got out, she peeked in the backyard and discovered the large oak tree with a kids' tire swing dangling from one of its thick branches. He opened his front door.

"You have a tree swing," said Penny.

"Yeah. It came with the house. I need to take it down but can't seem to do it. I want kids and a family someday."

Something squished around inside of her. She wanted kids and family, too. Not yet, but someday.

His living room smelled of fresh paint, but the couch was the same. The Michigan flag hung on the wall over the TV like in his condo.

Penny faced him and smirked at his maize and blue sweatshirt. "Still sporting the Michigan gear."

Beckett blushed. "Always and forever—Go Blue. Come on

in. Let's sit in the kitchen, I'm still sweaty from playing basketball."

He led her into his kitchen nook. "Coffee?"

"Sure."

Beckett ground beans and counted scoops into his coffee maker. "Drew told me you were in Nashville and Pittsburgh. I wanted to come to Misty Lake last week, but you weren't there."

"You did?"

"Yeah. I learned of your donation to *Ripple Effects*."

"It was the perfect place."

"Thank you. Helen is snickering in heaven, I'm sure." He handed her a cup of coffee and put some cookies onto a plate.

Penny took a sip of coffee and snagged a chocolate cookie. "Sorry about crashing into you. Again."

"It's alright. What were you doing at the park?"

"My plan was to visit you tomorrow, but I got in early and took a walk. You were on the court, but when you hugged the girl twice, I bolted. I assumed you had a new girlfriend."

Beckett shook his head and reassured her again, "She's my best friend's fiancée."

They sat in silence for a few minutes, and Penny ate another cookie. Beckett put his coffee mug down. "Penny, why are you here?"

Tears pooled in her eyes. "I went to Northern Woods and sat on the bench and listened to all of your messages. I was wrong to leave the way I did. We should've talked about the bribe and the trust and your relationship with your parents, but I thought if I disappeared from your life, it would be the best for everyone. I didn't want you to have to choose between me and your family's money."

Beckett picked up her hand, and the electric arc came alive

between them. Their eyes locked. "It ended up being an easy choice. I love the changes I've made."

"Tell me more about what you did after you left Boston."

"I dissolved the trust."

"Are you okay with that?"

"More than okay. I learned a little about love from Jackson and Helen, but you...you showed me unconditional love. Love wins every time."

Penny's eyes pooled.

"And I got rid of the plane. Commercial air travel sucks, by the way."

Penny grinned. "What about your parents?"

"I haven't heard from them, but Jackson visited. We went to a basketball game, and he's talking about retiring."

"Thank you for coming to my show and for the beautiful flowers."

"I wouldn't have missed it for anything. You worked so hard for it, and it showed. You were phenomenal. How's the gigging life?"

"Good. I gave notice to Drew, and I need to find a home base somewhere in the Midwest. Traveling from northern Minnesota isn't working for me. I'm thinking about joining the stage actor's union, too."

They chatted about the changes in their lives, and the sky darkened.

"How about some dinner?" Beckett asked.

"Sure."

Beckett made a pasta dish and opened a bottle of wine. They ate at his kitchen table and lingered over a second glass. After he cleared the plates, he clasped her hand, and fireworks exploded between them. Their fingers caressed each other until Beckett's eyes dilated. She left her seat and sat side-saddle on Beckett's lap. Penny brushed her hand along his jaw and pressed her lips against his. A tornado of wind blew through her ears, and stars lit up behind her eyes. She swiped Beckett's bottom lip with her tongue, and they engulfed each other. Her long legs straddled his lap, and she circled her arms around his neck. They kissed and kissed until Beckett carried her to his bed.

Beckett lay her on his bed and unbuttoned her shirt. When he splayed it open, he fingered the emerald resting in her cleavage. "You're still wearing the necklace."

"I never took it off." A long moment passed. "Make love to me," she whispered.

Chapter Thirty-Four

Soft snores woke Penny from her slumber, and her eyes adjusted to the daylight. Beckett lay on his back with his mouth open, deep in sleep. She crept out of bed to use the bathroom, and on the way back, her eye caught the framed photo on the wall. She grabbed Beckett's T-shirt off the floor and slipped it on over her head before sitting in the upholstered rocking chair.

The large framed photo of a solo loon on a lake was the most beautiful picture she'd ever seen. The playbill from her musical was stuck in the corner of the frame. A book sat on the end table beside her, and the strip of silly photos from the Love Snow Festival was the bookmark. Beckett's car keys lay beside the book, and the loon keychain was still attached. She rocked and stared at the photograph while tears streamed down her face. She hugged her knees and cried.

"Why are you sad?" asked Beckett from the bed.

"We wasted so much time being lonely loons."

He got up and pulled her back into bed. They faced each other, and he wiped her tears with the pad of his thumb. "We found our way back to each other."

They ushered in the morning with sweet love before it was time for Penny to leave for Pittsburgh. Beckett walked her to her car after breakfast. Penny clung to him, and he kissed her neck with his soft lips. His silky voice purred, "I'm so glad you came to see me."

"Me too. How about we give this another shot? I think Cincinnati would make a great home base for me. It's centrally located with lots of opportunities and...you're here."

Beckett smiled, and his double dimple winked at her. "I'm a better person with you in my life."

"Me, too."

"You won't miss the lakes?" he asked.

"I'll visit."

"Emma?"

"It's easy to keep in touch these days."

"Beth's coffee?"

"I'll find a new source."

He pulled a shiny silver key, attached to the loon keychain, out of his pocket and placed it in her palm. "Here's my house key. Take the north woods with you and come home soon."

"I love you," said Penny. She kissed Beckett one more time, until her legs wobbled like lake water. He held the car door open as she climbed inside. "See ya soon."

Epilogue

The curtain closed on another regional show. Penny didn't get the lead often, but she snagged it for the show in St. Louis and wore dark circles under her eyes to prove it. She dragged her butt back to the hotel and called Beckett.

"Home tomorrow?" he asked.

"Yeah."

"You've earned some time off."

The last eight months had been a whirlwind, but she didn't want to be anywhere else. Living with Beckett was fun and exhilarating—she even let her guard down and allowed him to help her from time to time. He helped her purchase a newer used car, and they spent one tense weekend organizing her finances. They split their expenses and were equal partners in their relationship.

Beckett traveled with her to some of her shows and worked remotely. She taught voice lessons when she wasn't on the road, and Beckett played basketball three times a week. The never-ending list of home improvement projects filled any remaining free time.

She secured an agent, joined the stage actor's union, and won part after part in regional musicals. It wasn't Broadway, but she made steady progress the last eight months.

"Flight lands at five. See ya tomorrow," said Penny.

Beckett wrapped her in his arms as soon as she walked through the front door. They'd been apart for weeks—she held him tight.

"Dinner is made, and the jacuzzi tub is full and waiting for you."

The primary room's bath was their first big home improvement splurge. The added jacuzzi tub was big enough for two, and they shared a soak before bed most nights. But today, Beckett left her alone to decompress. A silky chemise lay on the bathroom vanity for her, and she wondered if she'd have the energy for him.

Half an hour later, she emerged from the bathroom and crossed to their bed. Beckett handed her a glass of wine, and she climbed in beside him. The smooth liquid coated her throat, and she sighed. After a proper welcome home, they meandered downstairs.

"Sit. I'll bring us dinner."

She waited in the dining room while pots and pans clanged in the kitchen. He returned with two bowls of beef bourguignon and a basket of crusty bread. They ate and chatted, and he refilled her wine glass. After dinner, he said, "Let's go out into the backyard. I want to show you something before the sun sets."

They walked outside, and to the left of the tire swing, there was the bench from the Northern Woods shore.

Penny gasped and ran to the bench. "Did you buy it from Northern Woods?"

Beckett smiled and nodded. "I did. Don't worry, I purchased an exact replica and had it delivered to Northern Woods before they shipped this one to me."

She stared at the man who made every day worth living. "Why?"

"Because I love you and wanted a piece of Misty Lake and Northern Woods in our own backyard."

She lay her head on his shoulder and threaded her fingers with his while they listened to the night sounds of spring.

"Our first real conversation was on this bench," said Beckett.

"I remember," said Penny. "I prayed the whole time that you weren't going to yell at me for damaging your car."

He hugged her tight. "You gave me a piece of your brownie on this bench."

"You were so sad. I should've given you the whole thing."

"Nah."

"I taught you how to lace ice skates on this bench."

"I watched you twirl on the ice and couldn't take my eyes off you while sitting on this bench."

"Aww."

"Our first kiss was almost on this bench."

Penny chuckled. "No way was I going to let you kiss me for the first time in front of all those people."

"We watched a hockey game on this bench."

"It was sooo cold that day, remember?" Penny snuggled closer to him. "I listened to all of your messages on this bench." The sun set, and darkness engulfed the backyard.

Silence stretched between them, and all of a sudden, the backyard lit up with fairy lights. Tons of them. Lights strung from trees, across their patio, and over the rose bushes. Fairy lights blinked across the roof line of the house and along the fence.

Penny gasped at the twinkling yard. She clasped her hands over her mouth when Beckett dropped to one knee and opened a tiny velvet box in front of her. A sparkling, round diamond sat in the cushioned box.

"Penny O'Brien, you are the love of my life. You've helped me become a better person, a better lover, and a better friend. I want to spend the rest of my life with you. Will you marry me?"

Penny choked back a sob and nodded before whispering, "Yes, yes. I'll marry you, Beckett Young."

Acknowledgments

Thank you to Erin Helmrich and her amazing staff at the Fifth Avenue Press. A special thank you to Casey Gamble and Sara Peltier for their editing magic. I'm grateful to Nathaniel Roy for another fantastic cover and for all of your work on the interior layout. Thank you to Bryan Hood and Mandy Pas for diving into my rough draft as beta readers and giving me valuable feedback. Thank you to Shannon Locke for her theater and stage acting expertise and her willingness to answer all of my random questions! Finally, to my family and friends for supporting my efforts and cheering me on to the finish line. I appreciate and love you all.

About the Author

Amy Hepp fell in love with the Boundary Waters of northern Minnesota as a teenager and is excited to share this fiercely protected wilderness with her readers. Amy writes love stories set in the Boundary Waters from her screened-in porch among the birds and blue skies of Raleigh, North Carolina. When she's not writing, she enjoys running, working jigsaw puzzles, gardening, and visiting her three young adult children scattered across North America.

www.ingramcontent.com/pod-product-compliance
Lightning Source LLC
Chambersburg PA
CBHW031444200726
48289CB00007BB/2198